CINDERELLA'S JILTED BILLIONAIRE

by Lucy Monroe

1st Printing 2022

COPYRIGHT © 2022 LUCY MONROE

ISBN 9798362643027

ALL RIGHTS RESERVED

No part of this book may be reproduced, scanned, or distributed in any printed or electronic form without express, written permission from the author Lucy Monroe who can be contacted off her website http://lucymonroe.com.

This is a work of fiction. Names, characters, places, and incidents either are the product of the author's imagination or are used fictitiously, and any resemblance to actual persons, living or dead, business establishments, events, or locales is entirely coincidental.

Copyeditor: Z. Slawik

CINDERELLA'S JILTED BILLIONAIRE

Lucy Monroe

Lucy Monroe LLC

For Jadesola James, a new friend, a fabulous author, and someone who appreciates a good Cinderella story, but most importantly, loves a truly emotional romance. This story is for you and other authors and readers like you! Hugs!

Chapter One

Annette Hudson rushed around her tiny studio apartment, grabbing last-minute items. She was late leaving for the airport, but she'd had a last-minute emergency at work.

Nothing new in that. Understaffed and underfunded, her nonprofit organization expected her to wear multiple hats on a daily basis. Getting the week off for her little sister's wedding had been nearly impossible, but for once Annette had refused to back down about taking the time.

Joyce was getting married and Annette wasn't going to miss it. Not only was Joyce the only family who still had anything to do with her, but Annette was one of Joyce's bridesmaids. She had the dress to prove it.

That she would see the man she'd jilted at the altar five years before had nothing to do with the discordant concerto playing along her nerve endings. No, of course it didn't. He was just at the center of the biggest mistake of her life, costing her the family she'd dreamed of and the family she'd grown up with, not to mention the man she'd loved beyond reason.

Although the society pages showed him escorting a bevy of beautiful women to his mother's charity galas, Carlo Messina was still single. He would play best man for the groom. In a cruel twist of fate, Annette's baby sister had fallen for, and was marrying, Carlo's younger brother, Fantino Messina.

The similarities between the two couples were uncanny. Joyce was the same young twenty-two Annette had been when she'd left Carlo standing at the altar. Fantino was eerily the same age Carlo had been then as well, twenty-nine.

But there was no chance Joyce would take flight as Annette had done. Not only was she a far more self-assured twenty-two, confident in the love of her Sicilian tycoon, Joyce was also seven months pregnant. The plans had already been in place for the *wedding of the century* when Annette's younger sister told their families the happy news.

Their mother had been livid, but everyone else, even Carlo's conservative Sicilian relatives, had been delighted.

Annette was thrilled for her sister, if a little envious.

Joyce was building the very life that Annette had always dreamed of, and it was no one's fault but her own that she hadn't realized it first. Determined to show nothing but happiness for her sister, Annette rushed for the MAX line that would take her to the airport.

Several hours and a plane ride later, Annette dragged her suitcase out of the back of the taxi in front of an exclusive building in Manhattan. She might be willing to travel public transport in Portland, Oregon, but wasn't as confident of doing so alone in New York City.

You could take the girl away from wealth and privilege, but you couldn't stop the tapes playing in her head of all she'd been taught by parents who had a distinct *us and them* mentality when it came to the money *haves* and *have nots*. She didn't want to be afraid to ride the subway alone, but she was.

Would she ever be wholly her own person, leaving her parents' narrow view of the world behind completely?

She walked into the lobby of the apartment building and gave the doorman her name. Fantino had an apartment here and Annette was staying there for the week before the wedding. She could have stayed with her parents, but that would have been awkward when they hadn't had a real conversation in five years.

Not since her father had all but forced her to leave New York, by offering a substantial gift to her organization, if they transferred her to their office across country. She'd spent the last five years in exile, very pointedly not invited to family gatherings. Returning for a visit had been out of the question. Labeled an ungrateful daughter who had humiliated her family by standing her billionaire groom up at the altar, Annette had been shunned by everyone except Joyce since that fateful day.

Okay, so there could be a lot of reasons for the butterflies tap dancing in spiked cleats in her stomach right now, and Carlo Messina was only one of them.

The doorman requested her identification and then sent her up in the elevator to Fantino's penthouse floor. The man himself was there to greet her when she knocked on his door.

Looking so much like his older brother, it hurt her to see him, his teeth flashed white in a warm smile. "Annette! Welcome! Joyce will be so glad you have made it."

It was all Annette could do to summon a smile of acknowledgement to Fantino's words. She should have it together. She'd been wholly on her own since leaving New York. Annette had stood up to drug dealers who were messing with the kids in her program. She'd stared down cops doing the same thing.

The prospect of seeing Carlo Messina again shouldn't be so darn scary, much less her own parents.

Only it was.

She was shaking inside but hiding it, and that was the best she could hope for.

"Who is it?" Think of the devil and he will appear. Six feet, four inches of Sicilian male perfection, Carlo stood there looking amazing in a bespoke suit, his dark hair styled perfectly.

No pallor beneath his sun kissed skin to reveal nerves to rival hers. But then, he'd never actually loved her, and she'd never gotten over loving him. He hadn't had neatly trimmed facial hair six years ago. It gave him a sexy edge he didn't need. The man was already sex on a stick with a side of dark chocolate sauce.

The look in his grey eyes when they landed on her was indifferent. So much worse than anger. It indicated that while she hadn't been able to move on, he had.

"Oh, I see," he said dismissively. "Joyce is in the living room," Carlo turned to walk away.

Say something, she instructed herself, but Annette couldn't get a single word past the obstruction in her throat.

"Don't mind him. He's had enough girlfriends since you broke up, he can't claim he's been pining for you," Fantino said airily, leading her into the swank, modern living room of the penthouse.

If that was supposed to make her feel better, it had failed spectacularly.

"Annette!" Her sister's shout reached her ears only a second before the lithe brunette pulled her into a breath stealing hug.

Joyce was the only member of their family who called her by her full name, Annette. The rest of the family and extended family called her Netta, as if trying to erase the existence of her deceased birth mother, Anne.

"Isn't that sweet?" a smooth, feminine voice asked. Annette couldn't see the woman speaking through the crowd of well-wishers attending the prewedding party. "Only I thought Cinderella's family had disowned her."

Joyce let go of Annette and spun around. "The past is the past. My sister is one of my dearest friends and nothing will change that." It was like she was warning everyone in the room.

Annette knew Joyce had fought family pressure to maintain their relationship. Though the younger woman had said nothing, it must have been a battle royal when she insisted on inviting Annette to the wedding. Making her a bridesmaid would have been even worse in their parents' opinion.

Warmth and gratitude surged through Annette.

"Naturally not," Valentina Messina said smoothly as she arrived beside them, looking just as put together and lovely as Annette remembered the woman who had been meant to be *her* mother-in-law. "Family is family."

"Hello, Signora Messina," Annette said in a huskier tone than usual, but it was taking all she had to form words.

This was so much harder than she thought it would be.

The gorgeous woman now clinging to Carlo's arm like a limpet only made things worse.

Annette had never been a liar, so she'd never lied to herself and claimed to be over the man. She doubted she ever would be.

"It is Valentina, as I am sure you remember," the elegant older woman instructed. "So, you did not marry my eldest son." She waved negligently with her elegant hand. "Life has its little turns. However, your sister *will* be marrying my younger son and that is all that matters now."

Annette just nodded, all the time her focus inexorably drawn to the beautiful brooding man she had so foolishly walked away from five years ago.

"Thank you for the card and flowers when Alceu was in the hospital. The food baskets and coffee deliveries from my favorite barista were lovely," Valentina went on. "It was a kindness."

"I...it was the least I could do."

"What a kind thing to say, but under the circumstances untrue." She meant because Annette had no longer been a de facto member of the family. "His accident was such a worrisome time for us all and your thoughtfulness was very much appreciated." Valentina gave her husband a significant look. "I warned him for years to stop driving like he wanted to enter *Le Mans*. But would he listen?"

The weeks after her failed wedding were some of the hardest of Annette's life, made infinitely worse when Alceu, a man she'd come to love like a father, was in the car accident and was taken to the hospital. She could do nothing but watch from the sidelines, hoping he would recover.

The look on Carlo's face and her own parents' expressions said Valentina might be the only person who thought the way she did.

Though she'd had nothing to do with the accident, hadn't even been in the same country it happened in, they definitely blamed Annette. For all of it.

When Annette hadn't shown up at the church, the media had a heyday with their awful headlines and salacious innuendo laden articles and it only got worse after Alceu's accident. There had been speculation that, humiliated by his son being stood up at the altar and the subsequent media frenzy, Alceu had done it on purpose.

Cinderella Jilts Billionaire had morphed to *Even Billions of Dollars Can't Get Cinderella to the Altar*.

The whole Cinderella angle was her older sister's fault, not that anyone in her family would admit it. Lynette's friends used to make fun of Annette because more often than not, her mother would find fault with something about her appearance or behavior at a social function they were hosting and send Annette to the kitchen to help the cook or the serving staff.

She'd say if Annette couldn't handle her responsibilities as a daughter of the host, she might as well make some use of herself. Lynette's friends had dubbed her Cinderella and that's how that whole group referred to her on social media. Lynette had been the one to give an interview after the failed wedding to a gossip rag journalist about Annette, sharing the nickname and what a supposed failure Annette had been as a socialite.

Lynnette hadn't mentioned Annette's adopted status either, but then that would have sparked ire from their parents and Lynette was too smart for that. Only she hadn't been smart enough to realize that her words could be twisted, and they had been. Her family and Carlo had been raked over the coals by the press. They'd said that despite his billions, he was no Prince Charming.

Which was not true. He'd been her prince, she'd just been too insecure to realize it, much less fight for what they could have had.

Regardless of her lack of foresight, Lynnette had come out of the debacle smelling like a rose. As per usual. Completely ignoring her role in it, everyone had acted like it was Annette's fault the family had drawn censure for *making her into a modern-day Cinderella*.

It had taken two years of therapy for Annette to realize she had not been at fault. Yes, she'd jilted Carlo at the altar, and she could have handled that differently, but the media frenzy that ensued had not been on her. No matter what her family thought.

"Enough talking of the past, it is time to toast the happy couple," Alceu Messina announced with authority that would never leave him, no matter that he was officially retired now.

He'd worked hard coming back from his accident, and if she didn't know he'd spent six months in a hospital bed recovering from terrible damage to his body, she would never suspect it.

One toast followed another and soon the room was filled with laughing, chatting partygoers. If some gave Annette the side-eye, she ignored it. She was here for Joyce and that was what mattered.

Just as he had for the past six years, Carlo did a great job of ignoring Annette's existence. With his date always there, touching him and flirting with the Sicilian tycoon, Annette was happy to return the favor and kept her focus on Joyce, Fantino, and their friends that didn't seem interested in rehashing six years ago.

The rest of the week was more of the same. Annette spent the rehearsal doing her best to avoid looking at either Carlo, or her parents. It helped she was just a bridesmaid and not maid of honor. That position had been filled by their oldest sister, Lynette.

Annette didn't mind in the least. While she wasn't exactly an introvert, she really didn't like being the center of attention among this crowd, and Lynette's role meant she was the one giving the formal toast to the happy couple at the reception.

Annette didn't mind a bit when the youth she served focused on her. She was comfortable leading workshops for them, but that was different.

Carlo brought yet another beautiful companion to the rehearsal dinner, much to Lynette's obvious chagrin. Apparently, her older sister expected Carlo, as best man, to be her escort and complained to both sets of parents loudly enough to be overheard.

Annette would have found it all laugh worthy if she wasn't fighting her own jealousy over the date's presence. After five years, she should be more inured to such feelings, regardless of her feelings for the man.

After all, she had been strong enough to walk away when she realized it wasn't working. Which wasn't the show of strength she wanted to believe it was, because she doubted that decision almost every day, wishing she'd tried to at least talk to him again, wishing above everything she'd handled the cancelled wedding better.

Texting her parents and asking them to alert everyone else had been a colossal mistake.

Because of course they hadn't. They'd let everyone think she'd skipped town without a word to them. Why Carlo had shown up at the church when she'd told him to his face it was over, she didn't understand to this day.

Chapter Two

The wedding was beautiful. Joyce's Regency inspired gown had not been designed to hide her pregnancy and she glowed with joy from the moment she entered the church.

Annette could see not a single sign of wedding jitters.

The reception was held in one of the old grand hotel ballrooms, so exactly the way that Joyce had always said she wanted things to be, Annette couldn't help smiling. Though she was operating on her last reserves after a week of being her family's pariah and the recipient of censure from Carlo's extended family and friends.

His parents were wonderful, and of course so was his younger brother.

Carlo simply ignored her and that hurt most of all.

Done with it all, Annette had tucked herself into a corner of the ballroom away from everyone, just waiting for the bride and groom to leave so she could too.

"I cannot believe you were selfish enough to come to Joyce's wedding, Netta." Lynette's spiteful voice invaded Annette's solitude.

Sighing, Annette looked up. Lynette was glaring down at her. Nothing new there.

"Don't you have things you need to be doing as the matron of honor?" she asked.

"Can you believe our sister wanted to make you *maid* of honor?" Lynette asked derisively, as if the distinction between maid and matron was a negative one.

Annette didn't see it. Yes, Lynette had married since Annette left New York, but she had also divorced. That made them both single, if not technically *maids*.

Unlike Annette, Lynette had a busy social calendar though. She'd never landed the catch she really wanted to, however. Carlo Messina showed no more interest in Annette's older sister than he ever had. Despite being best man and Lynette being the matron of honor, Carlo had managed to finagle a change in the dance partner line up and Annette's sister had been stuck dancing with a cousin while Carlo had escorted his grandmother around the floor.

It had been the highlight of an otherwise miserable few hours for Annette, seeing her grasping older sister thwarted.

"I believe you owe me this dance," Carlo's voice startled both women.

Lynette turned, her expression going from sour to sweet in a heartbeat. "Do I?" she asked throatily.

But Carlo was looking at Annette, his hand extended to *her*.

Without really thinking of what she was doing, she reached out and took it.

He pulled her from her chair, the cornflower blue chiffon of her bridesmaid dress floating around her legs. The three-inch heels of her delicate silver strappy sandals bringing her petite height to average.

Lynette said, "Netta? But why would you want to dance with her?"

Carlo ignored the remark and pulled Annette toward the dance floor.

"What did Lynette ever do to you?" Annette asked as Carlo pulled her into his arms for a slow dance.

He looked at her like she had to be kidding. "She leaked that you broke things off. She's the one that got the whole media storm going in the first place, doing that tabloid interview."

"No one else blamed her."

"In her jealousy, she made an already difficult situation worse."

"My parents believe she was just trying to get ahead of the story, to protect the family, but it backfired."

"Your parents wear blinders where that one is concerned."

Annette agreed, but didn't realize anyone else saw the truth.

"So, you're mad she did the interview? But I'm the one that didn't show up at the church." Why had she said that? Why bring up her own culpability?

Because therapy had only increased Annette's need to live honestly. She'd hated the subterfuge and subtle untruths that permeated her childhood hiding her adopted status like it was something to be ashamed of.

"I am aware." With that, Carlo pulled her in close, making talking difficult.

Unless she wanted to speak into his shirtfront, Annette didn't complain. Her body was responding as it always did to his nearness and it was all she could to not to melt into him. She inhaled his delicious masculine scent, knowing this was probably the last time she would ever do so. She had no idea why he'd asked her to dance after avoiding her all week, especially if, as it seemed, he didn't want to talk.

He still wore the cologne she'd picked out for him while they were dating. She wondered why. Did he like it that much? He had to overlook his antipathy toward the first person to have bought it for him every time he put it on. Or had he simply forgotten it was her?

What a demoralizing thought.

Soon any thought of cologne or gifts floated right out of her head as controlling her libido became her overriding concern. Desire bloomed deep in her belly and spread throughout her body so that everywhere they touched zinged with the electric current of need.

One song bled into another and rather than let her go, Carlo simply pulled her that much closer. Close enough that she could tell the dancing was having the same effect on him as it did on her.

"You want me," she whispered in shock.

He chuckled darkly, like he was laughing at himself. "We often want what is not good for us."

"We should..." she made a feeble attempt to step back.

He held her firmly. "Continue dancing, I agree."

He separated their bodies only when the music had shifted to something with a faster beat. Annette looked around them and realized he'd maneuvered them away from the crowded dance floor, toward the back of cavernous ballroom.

"We must have looked ridiculous dancing back here by ourselves." Not that Annette really cared about things like that.

"I doubt anyone even noticed."

Catching the glare of both her sister Lynette, and their mother, Annette had to disagree. Even Joyce was looking at them, but she was giving Annette the thumbs up and grinning.

Going on the principle that if she couldn't see them, her mom and oldest sister couldn't ruin the moment, Annette smiled back at Joyce and then turned so the only person she could see was Carlo.

"Why did you dance with me?" she asked baldly.

"Because I want you."

She stared. How was she supposed to respond to that? With honesty. She wasn't a naïve virgin, neither was he. "I want you too."

He passed her a black and gold keycard. "I have a suite here. Meet me there after Fantino and Joyce have had their sendoff."

Annette took the keycard automatically, but then immediately regretted doing so and tried to shove it back at him. "No. I can't. What about your girlfriend?"

"I do not have a girlfriend. I had a date."

"Had?"

"I sent her home in a car."

"Won't she be angry?"

He shrugged. "Perhaps, perhaps not. She got entrée to the event and the chance to make the connections she wanted."

"You're saying she only dated you for the access you could provide her? I don't believe that."

"The sex was a bonus," he said cynically.

Annette winced. It hurt to hear that cynicism in his voice, but it hurt even more to think about him having sex with another woman.

"You don't like the idea of me in bed with her."

"No." Again, honesty was her only fallback. Not a naïve virgin, but a possessive ex. She'd like to sink through the floor as she acknowledged that maybe honesty was not *always* the best policy.

"Then, you be that woman tonight."

"You're not some playboy who has a different bed partner every night."

"You sound very sure about that."

"It's not who you are."

"It has been five years. You don't know who I am."

"You could be right." She would have turned to leave, but something in his expression arrested her. "You want to make love with me, tonight."

"I want sex with you, *sì*."

Annette really didn't care what terminology they used. If they joined their bodies, emotion would be involved. Whether he acknowledged that emotion, or not, didn't mean it wouldn't be there.

The question was, could she live with all the emotion being on her side?

She'd spent five years unable to get over him. Maybe having sex with him without any commitments or even the tenuous tie of dating would give her what she needed to move on.

Closure.

They said that if what you were doing wasn't working, then you should change it. Being deprived of his company for five years hadn't given her the ability to let him go, but maybe this would.

Besides, Annette's body was already at nuclear meltdown levels, just from dancing with him. She'd been celibate so long, she hadn't bothered to have her IUD replaced when the time had come to remove it. Her body craved what her heart told her only he could give her.

By tomorrow morning, maybe both of those things would have shifted.

Determined to see through the sensual promise in his expression, she nodded to herself. "All right."

His gorgeous eyes flared infinitesimally, like she'd surprised him.

Annette tucked the keycard away in a hidden pocket in her dress and headed back into the ballroom.

Carlo watched Annette walk away from him, her honey blonde hair coming down from its formal updo, her beautiful curvy body moving enticingly in her blue dress, and wondered if he'd just made the biggest mistake of his life.

He'd known since sending Cynthia home that he was going to do it.

Annette had made it easy, but even if she hadn't, Carlo knew he would have pursued her with everything in his arsenal. Because he wanted what his brother had. A wife who wanted children with him. A wife who wanted to raise those children herself and not leave it up to others.

Someone unlike his own mother. As much as Carlo loved her, he wanted a mother for his children who would make time in *her* life for them.

And he wasn't going to find that until he'd worked Annette Hudson out of his system. Five years. It had been five years since she had jilted him, made him the butt of every kind of joke.

And in those years, Carlo had had sex with exactly two other women, one time each. On both occasions he'd been left feeling hollow and unsatisfied, regardless of the physical climax they'd both achieved. He could not forget the way it felt to make love to Annette.

He still dreamt about the woman who had as good as thrown his ring back in his face.

After the debacle, she'd sent the custom-made diamond and sapphire engagement ring back via her father. Carlo still had it stored in his wall safe. Maybe he could get rid of it after he finally got her out of his system.

Because he wasn't just being pedantic, he intended to have sex with her tonight, not make love. And in so doing, exorcise the demons that would not let him go.

The rest of the reception was a blur for Annette. She couldn't stop thinking about what was going to happen after. She'd meant to return to her spot out of the way, but Joyce had called Annette over, insisting she take Lynette's empty matron of honor seat.

"Lynette isn't going to be happy if she comes back and finds me here."

"I don't understand why she resents you so much," Joyce said with a familiar younger sister eyeroll. "You always did everything she didn't want to, making her life easier."

And been made into a meme because of it.

"Mom was lucky you were so accommodating. Lynette never would have been," Joyce said warmly.

She called Annette *Cinderella* with affection, finding it a great joke. She would never understand how much all the publicity that had circulated around Annette getting that moniker had hurt. Joyce had been a sunny dispositioned teen when it had happened and Annette wasn't about to go into old hurts now.

"I saw you with Carlo."

"I know." Annette shook her head. "Don't go getting romantic ideas. That man despises me."

"It sure didn't look like he hated you when you were dancing."

It hadn't felt like it either, but Annette knew something Joyce didn't seem to want to realize. When the sex happened, it wasn't going to be because Carlo wanted to start again with Annette.

They'd always been sexually compatible. Combustible more like.

The sex had been amazing, and Annette thought Carlo just wanted some more of it. Five years ago, she'd mistaken amazing sex for love, but she wouldn't make that mistake again.

She was looking for closure.

Nothing more.

If her heart accused her of lying to herself, Annette ignored that too savvy inner voice.

She had a keycard to his room, and she intended to use it.

Chapter Three

Annette stood outside the hotel room door, her palms sweaty, and her heart beating a mile a minute.

Was she really going to go through with this? Was she going to have sex with Carlo Messina, when they hadn't spoken before this week in five years?

He'd refused all her attempts at communication, blocking her email address, her phone number, and on social media. He'd wanted nothing to do with her and she was sure that would have continued if their siblings hadn't fallen in love and decided to marry.

So, what was she doing here?

Getting her own closure and maybe giving him some too, not that he acted like he needed it. But if he did? She owed it to him. Not via sex, that was her choice, but if she could give him closure too, she wanted to.

Sure, and you aren't trying to rekindle anything. That heart voice was back, and it was laced with sarcasm.

Ignoring it, Annette lifted the keycard toward the door, but still she hesitated.

A sound down the corridor decided her. The one thing she was certain of was that she did not want to be caught standing outside his door.

She passed the keycard over the electronic reader and the door clicked. Taking a deep breath and letting it out, she opened it.

Annette stopped stock still at the sight that greeted her, the door swishing shut behind her.

Carlo was already inside, reclining naked on the bed, his dark hair wet from the shower. He had a drink in his hand. It looked like the Scotch malt whiskey he favored in a rock glass.

"You look like you've seen a ghost."

She shook her head, mute with overwhelming desire.

He put his hand out to her. "Come here."

"I'm still dressed." She'd found her voice. Just barely.

"Then allow me the privilege of undressing you."

So similar to things he'd used to say all the time to her, the words triggered a visceral reaction in Annette, her eyes stinging with emotion.

Carlo stood, his body rippling with even more muscles than she remembered. He'd always been well formed, but now he was really fit, his skin glowing with health.

"Do you work out a lot more?" she asked inanely.

He did not seem to mind, giving her a slashing smile. "Maybe. Are you saying I'm in better shape than I was five years ago?"

She licked suddenly dry lips. "Your muscles are more defined."

"And you like that?"

She nodded, incapable of speech.

He started by pulling the pins from her updo, allowing her long hair to completely release from its confinement. He took some of her long honey-colored curls between his fingers, seemingly mesmerized by the sight. "Your hair used to be darker."

"Lowlights." Annette had been getting brown streaks added to her honey blonde hair since she was an adolescent. Her mom had suggested them, and Annette had been desperate to fit in with her adopted family, so she'd gone along.

No amount of hair dye was going to make her part of the Floyd Hudson family, but she hadn't understood that until she was in Portland, letting her own blond roots grow out.

Carlo touched her natural blonde hair like he was rubbing silk between his fingers. "I like this better."

"I do too." And that was all that mattered anymore. Annette had given up all vestiges of trying to fit into her adopted family when she was exiled from New York.

"You are so different from the rest of your family," he mused, like he was just now making that observation.

Annette just shrugged. They'd never talked about the fact she was adopted. Her parents treated that fact like it was a state secret, and therefore so had Annette.

If tonight led to anything more, she would tell Carlo the truth of her past. It might help him understand her actions six years ago.

Though she wasn't counting on it. It had taken two years of therapy for Annette to understand herself.

And why was she thinking like that? This was closure, no matter what her inner voice said.

"Stop," he instructed as he unzipped the back of her dress.

She shivered in anticipation of what was to come. "What?"

"Thinking."

"No thinking?" she asked, perplexed. When had thinking become a bad thing?

"Only feeling. Only pleasure. Only me."

Ah, so he wanted her focus on him. That she could do. "Only you."

He tugged her dress off, letting it pool in a cloud of blue chiffon around her feet. She wore only a pale blue bra and panties set she'd bought just to wear under the bridesmaid dress.

"I like these." He touched the tiny pink rosettes where her bra cups met with a fingertip. "But I like these best of all." He cupped her lush breasts, brushing his thumbs over her nipples poking against the delicate silk.

Pleasure zinged a direct path from her tightened peaks to her core.

He leaned down and put his mouth over the blue silk, gently nipping and then sucking her nipple through the thin fabric.

Bombarded by sensations she hadn't felt in years, Annette shuddered. She'd tried sex with other men, but had balked at the final hurdle. Their kisses never felt right. Their touch felt too alien on her skin. Ultimately, she simply couldn't share her body with them.

She'd talked to her therapist about that too.

The revelation that she still loved Carlo had not been surprising. Her therapist's suggestion that she give her heart and body all the time she needed to move on had shocked her as it was so antithetical to how her family expected her to handle emotion. Learning that being told to simply forget one father while embracing her uncle as her dad was not in fact okay, had been freeing. Being told by someone that she could take all the time she needed to move on from Carlo had been too.

Annette had stopped trying to be what her family said she should and had simply accepted being herself.

Being herself had gotten her here and that wasn't so bad at all.

Heat suffused her body as he continued stimulating her breasts through the silk of her bra. Suddenly he cupped her bottom with both hands, lifted her, and carried her to the bed.

She landed on her back looking up at Carlo in all his primal masculine glory.

His pupils were blown, his expression dark with sexual need, his big body glowing in the lamplight of the room.

He reached out and touched the rosette right above her feminine mound. "So pretty."

"I like pretty underwear."

"I know." He gave her a slashing grin filled with sexual heat. "I like how they hint at your feminine beauty."

She always used to demur when he said stuff like that, telling him she knew she wasn't beautiful. Now, she soaked it in.

He smiled again. "No denial? I like that too."

"I've matured."

He didn't reply but slid his hands up her thighs and took hold of her underwear waistband. "All right?"

She nodded, wanting to be naked with him more than she'd ever wanted anything in her life, including her parents' affection and approval.

He tugged the blue silk down her thighs slowly, using the time to amp up the sexual tension between them. Annette reached behind herself to unclasp her bra, wanting it off as well.

"Impatient?" Carlo teased as he *finally* tugged her panties over her feet and tossed them on the floor behind him.

"Aren't you?" she taunted back.

"Maybe, but I'm going to savor you, Annette. We have all night."

She flung her bra aside. "I don't want to wait all night to have you inside me."

He didn't make her wait that long, but at times it felt like it. Carlo was on a mission to taste and touch every inch of her body, to drive Annette to a gibbering, pleading mess.

Finally, done with the teasing and the slow seduction, she pushed him onto his back. "Condom?" she asked in a tone that she hoped let him know she was done playing.

He grabbed one from under the pillow and Annette put it on him, her hands shaking. But she got it. And then, she took him into her body.

Her climax came almost immediately, causing her body to bow backward and a raw scream to erupt from her throat.

Carlo wasn't done though. He flipped their bodies, setting a slow pace of deep thrusts that aroused her all over again. By the time she climaxed the second time, he was pistoning into her body and shouting his own release.

Afterward, he got rid of the condom, but it was obvious he wasn't done.

"More?" she asked, a little awed.

He'd been a keen lover six years ago, but this was like pent up need finally finding an explosive outlet. She knew he hadn't been celibate. He'd been featured in too many gossip rags with sexy, beautiful women over the past years.

However, something was driving him, and she was happy to go along for the ride, finally falling into an exhausted sleep somewhere near dawn.

Annette woke feeling more comfortable in her skin than she had in years. Maybe ever.

Even five years ago, she had held parts of herself back from Carlo, afraid that if he knew the real her, he would lose interest. She'd still been dying her hair, dressing like her social set and socializing with the *right* people.

It was a lot more than her hair that had changed in the intervening time.

Annette's friends were more social activists now than socialites. She spent her spare time marching and organizing for her causes. She'd rather read than play tennis, and hike rather than play golf. She ate at food trucks and family-owned restaurants, instead of the latest hot spot with a Michelin Star.

She couldn't help wondering how the *new* Annette was going to fit in with Carlo's life. He came from wealth and privilege that far exceeded her own.

Refusing to let worry cloud her sense of wellbeing, she opened her eyes.

Annette was not surprised to be in the bed alone. Carlo had never needed as many hours of sleep as she did. The only times she'd ever woken with him beside her, he'd been up and working, only to return to bed to make love.

So, the empty bed and bedroom was no surprise. Annette got up and took a shower, a little surprised when the sound of hot running water hadn't brought her highly sexual lover into the bathroom. He must be on a business call.

She took her time drying her hair before donning one of the suite's complimentary robes to go in search of Carlo.

Annette cautiously looked through the cracked door as she opened, not wanting to be caught in the camera lens of a video call in a hotel bathrobe.

The living room was empty though. There was a cold breakfast of pastries and juice on the coffee table, obviously left there for her as the clear plastic dome was still over the plate of mouth-watering pastries. No note, but breakfast itself was a message.

Carlo was taking care of her.

No doubt still very much a workaholic, he must have gotten called away on business.

Annette sat down and uncovered the pastry plate, suddenly ravenous. She inhaled a perfectly flaky croissant filled with berries and cream before pouring herself a cup of coffee from the thermos style carafe. The dark liquid smelled divine and still steamed before she added milk and sugar.

Annette found her dress and the secret pocket that still had her cell phone in it. She used it to call his number.

He picked up on the third ring. "Hello?"

"It's Annette." She couldn't expect him to still have her number in his phone. They hadn't called each other in more than half a decade.

"Yes?"

"If you were expecting me to save you some pastry, you might be out of luck," she joked. "They're delicious."

"I have already eaten."

"Of course you have. What time did you get up anyway?"

"Does it matter? Did you need something, Annette?"

The coolness of his tone finally registered. This wasn't about talking in front of business associates. This was about how he was responding *to her*.

"You were gone when I woke up," she pointed out, but at what point last night had she decided he would be there?

When had she shifted from seeking closure to looking for something more?

"Naturally."

His neutral tone was getting to her. "You didn't leave a note."

"Why would I have?"

"Um, because that would have been polite?"

"I wasn't aware that there was an etiquette for one-night stands."

All the air whooshed out of Annette's lungs like she'd been sucker punched. "What do you mean?" she forced out.

Okay, he'd said it was just sex before it even started, but did that mean he couldn't treat her with common decency? Is this how men and women who had one-night stands treated each other?

If it was, she was glad she'd been celibate. Annette didn't like it. At all.

She'd had enough of being treated like an afterthought that didn't matter by her family.

"We weren't starting something last night, Annette. If anything, we were finally finishing it."

"Last night was closure for you?" she asked through suddenly dry lips, envious if it was true.

She'd wanted to give him closure if she could, but she'd also wanted it for herself and the way she'd woken up this morning thinking about a future with him was proof she, at least, hadn't gotten it.

"*Sì.*" Which was an admission that he'd needed closure.

That was something, what she wasn't sure, but something.

"A one-night stand," she reiterated.

"*Sì.*"

"I've never had one," she mused mostly to herself.

He made an odd sound. "Now you have."

"Carlo..." Her voice trailed off. She didn't know what she wanted to say to him.

"If that is all?" But he didn't sound as unmoved as he had earlier.

It was almost like he needed to get off to the phone.

"You left me breakfast." Why had he done that?

"It seemed the polite thing to do."

Ah, manners. Carlo had impeccable ones. And apparently, he knew what was called for these situations. Unlike her. "So, there is an etiquette for one-night-stands, only I didn't know."

"We had great sex last night, Annette. I wouldn't mind repeating the experience, but that is all it was."

"You wouldn't mind repeating the..." Oh, the arrogant so-and-so!

She'd blast him, but the truth was, Annette couldn't be entirely sure that if he asked, she'd say no. She'd walked into this hotel room with both eyes open.

But then they'd started kissing and touching and nothing about that had been emotionless. "It wasn't just physical pleasure, for either of us." He could acknowledge it, or not.

The truth was the truth.

"Perhaps not. We do share a past."

"Last night we shared a lot more than a past." They'd shared their bodies in every imaginable way. "You couldn't get enough of me."

And if she knew him at all, he'd left that morning, so he didn't give into the temptation of having her again. Because he might not trust her, but he still wanted her, and closure wasn't sex until you literally could not stop collapsing from exhaustion.

That was wanting more.

Only he had no intention of admitting it, did he?

"Thank you for breakfast," she said as he began to say something. "I'll see you around."

But she fervently hoped not before she'd developed some defensive walls where he was concerned.

Annette was not built for one-night stands.

She hung up before he could reply. When her phone rang a few minutes later, she ignored it.

However, she read the text that came in a few seconds after the call went to voicemail.

It isn't polite to hang up on people.

She texted back. *I thought one-night stands didn't need to be polite.*

I left you breakfast.

Yes, he had, but he'd also left her with the painful realization that Annette was no closer to being over Carlo than she had been before their wild night of lovemaking.

Chapter Four

Annette refused to pick up when Carlo called, but she replied to his texts.

Sometimes he sent ones laden with sexual innuendo, other times he sent her memes that made her laugh out loud. Some were just comments about his day.

They didn't text every day, but a full week did not go by before he would reach out again.

He always initiated the communication. It was her rule.

It felt right after spending five years being blocked by him, which she noticed was no longer an issue. She'd never unfriended Carlo on social media platforms and suddenly his posts started showing up in her newsfeeds.

He also reacted to her posts, which led to one spectacular donation for the summer youth camp she organized.

Were they *friends* now? She wasn't sure, but it seemed like it.

Apparently closure for Carlo meant they could be friends. But those sexy texts? They implied he wanted more.

Annette just wasn't sure what she wanted.

Annette flew to New York as soon as she could get a flight when her sister went into labor and made it in time to be in the room when Jocinda Valentina Messina was born. Her name filled Annette with warmth since her sister had told Annette that she and Fantino had agreed to name their daughter after both Joyce and Annette, using a derivative of the nickname Joyce still called Annette in their private calls and texts. Cinderella.

For once the moniker brought nothing but pleasure to Annette.

Joyce was euphoric after the birth of her daughter and Annette hated having to leave that much happiness to return to Portland, but she'd been recently promoted to regional director for her organization, and it could not be helped.

A month later, she flew to Sicily for the christening, and was shocked at her sister's wan appearance and Fantino's unhappy demeanor.

Annette waited until they were alone together on the terrace overlooking the pool and a fabulous view of the Mediterranean at the Messina family mansion to approach Joyce about it. "Is everything okay, honey?"

Everyone had congregated for a celebratory lunch and the grandmothers were currently taking turns holding the little sleeping Jocinda, cooing over the baby and saying what a sweetheart she was.

"What do you mean?" Joyce asked defensively, her wan face pinched. "Of course, it is."

"You and Fantino look a little worn, is all," Annette said soothingly. "Can I help?"

"With you living across country? What are you going to do, rock my daughter to sleep via video call?" Joyce's derisive tone took Annette aback.

"I could come stay if you want me to."

"I'm fine. My baby is fine. I can handle it," Joyce said with more anger than confidence, turning and storming to the other side of the terrace.

She pressed her hands on the rail, her grip so tight Annette could see the whites of her knuckles from where she stood in worried bewilderment.

"Trust you to upset your sister on such a special day." Her mother's voice had Annette spinning around.

Annette took a deep breath and let it out before speaking. "I wasn't trying to upset her."

"Not to be too indelicate, but you need to butt out, Netta. Your sister is fine."

The woman who had just snapped at her and looked like she hadn't slept in a week was not fine. "I guess we don't see the same thing when we look at her."

"No, we don't. I am not jealous of what she has."

The accusation hit too close to the bone for Annette to respond immediately. She wasn't jealous of her sister, but she'd had moments of envy she'd had to work through. Her therapist said that was normal, but Annette still felt guilty about it.

Without another word, Annette's mother walked away.

Typical. Why try to have a conversation with the daughter you barely acknowledged? If it wasn't for Joyce, Annette was pretty sure her family would simply have stopped acknowledging her all together.

"That didn't sound good." Carlo's concerned tone coming from behind her had Annette spinning around.

She'd seen him from a distance at the Christening, but had managed to avoid talking to him until now.

She frowned at him. "I wasn't being nosy. I'm concerned."

"Did I say anything?" he asked, his hands up in that gesture that meant he wasn't guilty.

Realizing she was reacting to her mother's words and not his, Annette felt heat steal up her neck. "I am sorry, I should not have snapped at you."

"What was that all about?" he asked, waving away the apology.

"Have you noticed that your brother barely smiles and that my sister looks like she hasn't slept in a week?" she asked, unable to believe she was the only one who saw how beleaguered both new parents had become.

However, Carlo flicked his hand dismissively. "New parenthood is hard. It is to be expected."

"You say that like you know something about it, but you don't have any children." And his mother had always had help, so Annette doubted sincerely this attitude was coming from Valentina or Alceu Messina.

"No, I don't. The woman who promised me marriage and a family left me standing at the altar." He said it sardonically, with little emotion, but the anger banked in his gaze said all she needed to know about how much he'd forgiven her.

Which was not at all.

Despite their night of uninhibited passion after their siblings' wedding and the texting and online *friendship* they'd built since then. It would be smart of her to remember that.

"Okay, so neither of us is parents. Noted. That doesn't change the fact that they need our help." How could he not see that?

"I could offer to hire a nanny for them, but my brother is perfectly capable of doing so. I am unclear on what kind of help you hope to offer?" he asked, reflecting her sister's attitude almost verbatim.

"I could go and stay with them if they need me," she said, repeating what she'd told Joyce.

The look Carlo gave her was odd. "You realize that would require you taking time off of work. I thought you were busy with the new regional directorship."

"I did not say it would be easy, but I could do it."

"If you were needed." There was something in Carlo's tone. It wasn't quite derogatory, but it was something. He shrugged. "Look, If Joyce needs help, your mother is there in New York for her to call on."

"My mother isn't going to offer to babysit." But honestly, Annette wasn't sure that was true. "Okay, maybe she will. She loves Joyce after all."

Unlike the adopted daughter she'd taken on sufferance.

"So, you have nothing to worry about."

Only that everyone else seemed to think how wan her sister looked was normal and okay.

Maybe Annette was being paranoid and feeling guilty because she wasn't in town and able to offer real help with the baby. Her sister was right. Annette couldn't rock her baby niece to sleep, or help by changing a diaper, or in any other tangible way from across the country.

Unlike the rest of her family, she wasn't wealthy and couldn't pay for once a week help for her sister to get a break, or anything like *that* either.

Perhaps the time had come to move back to New York. If her father balked, Annette would tell him to deal with it. She'd lived in exile long enough. She had stayed away for over five years. Surely that was enough time for the embarrassment her actions had brought her family to have subsided and her notoriety with it.

She couldn't afford to live in the city, even if she left the nonprofit sector, which she didn't want to do. But she could move close enough to make it possible to see her sister weekly, instead of only for the major events in Joyce's life.

"You don't look like you are getting much sleep yourself," Carlo remarked.

He didn't sound concerned exactly, but he didn't sound like he was reveling in her misfortune either.

"Jetlag," she dismissed, though she knew that was only part of it.

She hadn't been sleeping well for weeks. Her promotion had been eye opening in some very negative ways.

Now that Annette had access to what all the employees in her region were being paid, the realization that there were gross inequities in pay for marginalized staff had hurt. Finding out that she was not allowed to address those inequities because of national policy for the organization had been soul destroying.

She was currently fighting for pay raises for three of the employees and the amount of red tape being thrown her way opened her eyes to realities she found beyond unacceptable.

"How long will you be in Sicily?" he asked, speculation in his grey eyes.

"Just three days."

"That is a rather short stay for such a long flight."

He was right. Flying commercial from Oregon made for an extremely long day flying, especially when she'd had a four-hour layover in Rome because her flight to Sicily had been delayed. The flight home would be worse. "I couldn't take any more time off from my job."

Disappointment flashed in his grey gaze. "Ah, yes, your career comes first."

He didn't point out the fact that if she wanted to help her sister in any meaningful way, Annette's job could not take the precedence it always had. They both knew it and clearly, he believed she wouldn't make the necessary changes.

Why should he think any differently? Annette had refused to change jobs to move to Sicily with him after their wedding. Looking back, especially knowing what she did now about her organization, regret sat heavily on her heart.

"It's all I have right now," she admitted baldly. Particularly if Joyce didn't *want* Annette's help or presence.

Annette had no social life to speak of. All of her friends were from work and their socialization happened around work. Her new position was making her take stock of how the management expected that kind of commitment from employees that were not paid enough to make rent and utilities without a partner.

Like her. She'd had to sell stuff and work a seasonal second job to make ends meet.

"Being named our niece's godparent meant nothing to you then?" he asked, this time the disappointment in her was easy to see.

"That's not what I said. I just..." Being named Jocinda's godparent wasn't going to change Annette's life appreciably.

Not as long as she kept living in Portland.

Joyce was the only member of Annette's family who wanted anything to do with her, but she lived across country. They video chatted weekly, and Annette had been able to return to New York for important events, like Joyce's wedding and Jocinda's birth, but it wasn't enough.

Annette could only see one way to fix that.

Carlo stepped closer to her, leaned down and spoke in that low tone that sent shivers through her. "You just what?"

"Oh no you don't." She hurriedly stepped back, her progress blocked by the railing. She put her hand up in the *stop* gesture. "You stay over there."

"What is the matter, Annette?" Carlo had remained in her personal space, his body giving off pheromones that hers reacted to regardless of what her mind insisted she do.

Do not give in. Leave him alone. Steer clear of his brand of Sicilian seduction.

"You've got that look in your eye," she accused.

"What look is that?" he asked, stepping forward again so her hand pressed against his chest.

How had he gone from being disappointed in her, to wanting sex with her? What did that say about him wanting her at all? That he was only interested in her body and not the mind of the woman he didn't understand.

"You know what I'm talking about, and we aren't going there."

He tugged her hand up to his mouth and tickled her palm with the tip of his tongue, sending shivers down her arm and to places more intimate. "I think we should." He kissed her palm.

Desire burst into flame inside her so potent her knees wanted to buckle. Annette gripped the rail behind her and stood firm. This was not happening.

"I'm not one-night stand material," she told him tightly.

He gave her a devilish smile. "How about friends with benefits?"

"We aren't friends."

"Aren't we?" he asked with amusement. "You know me better than anyone, surely that makes us friends."

"*Friendship* makes friends, and we don't have that." Only, they sort of did.

Now.

"I text you more often than I do anyone else. We follow each other on social media."

Now they did. "For five years, you wouldn't take a single call or text or email."

"I was angry. My Sicilian emotions run deep."

"Are you saying you've forgiven me?"

"I am saying I want to spend the time you have here in Sicily together."

"In bed."

"And out of it."

Annette went still. *That* was different.

"And when I go back to Portland?"

"I've never tried sexting, but I'm game."

"No," she said quickly, before her own temptation to indulge in both suggestions that sounded wildly interesting showed on her face. "I'm not wired for casual sex."

Which she knew was true, but she also knew that sex with Carlo would never be casual for her, at least.

"Isn't that old fashioned?" He brushed her nape, sending frissons of enticement traveling along her nerve endings. "What about the sexual revolution women have fought so hard for?"

That was rich coming from one of the original throwbacks. "It's about having the freedom to have sex, or not, as we see fit, Carlo. Not a mandate to have sex."

"You do want me," he said with conceited assurance.

That was unfortunately entirely justified.

"But I don't want no-strings sex."

He stepped back, a cloak of cold withdrawal going around him. "I'm not offering strings to you."

"I didn't think you were." Which was why, this time, Annette was thinking with her head and not her sexual desire, or her heart. "You made that abundantly clear the last time."

"So, you refuse to give into what we both want because I know better than to trust you with anything other than sex?" His tone said he couldn't quite believe his ears.

She wanted to shout, *Welcome to the club, buddy!*, but asked instead, "You don't think you can trust me?" She made no attempt to hide her own shock.

"How can you be surprised by that?" He stared down at her, that disbelief now written clearly on his handsome features. "You left me standing at the altar."

"I told you I wouldn't be there." She still didn't understand why he'd shown up.

"I thought it was prewedding jitters. I made the mistake of trusting you to keep your promise and all that got me was public and private humiliation and vilification," he said with grim judgement.

Carlo had really believed she would show up at the church. That just boggled her mind.

Was it because he'd believed in their relationship that strongly, or simply could not imagine her refusing to fall in with his plans?

"You wouldn't listen to me, not about the honeymoon, not about moving. It took too long for me to realize that there were compromises we could have made, that we needed to talk more." How many times had Annette wished over the last seven and a half years she'd gone through with the wedding and then offered up those options, or at least insisted on discussing them beforehand?

"Compromises?" he asked with scorn, the usual urbane charmer no longer in evidence. "Your actions showed you weren't interested in compromising in any way."

She could see why he thought that. She'd told her parents the wedding was off after trying to give Carlo back her ring. Then she'd run away. She'd turned off her phone and found a no name motel to hole up in. She hadn't even realized the media frenzy was happening until it was too late to do anything meaningful to mitigate it.

By then Alceu had his accident and Floyd Hudson had already spoken to the head office of her organization, making an offer they had no intention of refusing. Her transfer had happened in a matter of days. "I am truly sorry. There are reasons—"

"There is no excuse for you running away like you did," he said adamantly.

"I didn't say excuses, I said reasons. And honestly, even understanding myself better now, after the highhanded way you planned our future and the length of our honeymoon without consulting me, I'm not sure I could have done anything differently." That had been a hard thing to acknowledge.

Almost as hard as realizing she had reacted more to the fear of being rejected than what he'd said and done.

It was a conundrum she'd never quite found a solution to. She knew her reaction had been knee-jerk and over the top, but even knowing that she should have pressed for another talk with him, she could not be confident that the end result would have been any different.

As much as she'd wished over and over that she'd gone through with the wedding, she'd also thought an equal number of times she'd been right to call it off. Not how she'd done it maybe and not because she was afraid of him eventually dumping her because she wasn't the perfect woman for him, but because their relationship had been too unequal.

She'd been too used to unequal relationships to see it. Then anyway.

Now, she saw the past through a very different lens than the one she'd used to look at life through when she was twenty-two. Which did not mean they couldn't have found more even footing to stand on.

Was that why she found it so hard to let him go? The unknown of whether they could have worked things out, or not?

"Good to know your apology just now was as sincere as your promise back then." Carlo turned and walked away, but unlike Joyce, he headed back inside the traditional Mediterranean style mansion.

Annette didn't call him back.

She was too busy reliving the conversation that had prompted her to call off the wedding.

Chapter Five

"So, we'll take two months, using a house on the Dalmatian Coast as our base, and my new yacht, exploring every bit of ancient culture in Croatia, Italy, Greece and Turkey that we can." Wealthy Sicilian tycoon, Carlo finished speaking and looked at Annette with expectation in his grey gaze, like he'd just offered her the world, not tried to take hers apart.

"I can't take two months off for a honeymoon," she told him, quite reasonably she thought, when really? She wanted to scream.

At 22, she'd only graduated university the year before and she'd landed her dream job as a program coordinator for an organization that serviced youth in the Foster Care system.

His handsome face settled into a frown. "But you love travel and history. It is the perfect honeymoon for you, *bèdda mia*."

For once, Annette didn't react to him calling her *his beauty* in Sicilian. She could not let herself get sidetracked by the way he made her feel. She loved him more than anything else and still, something inside her was screaming a warning because of his words.

This was too important. "And if you were talking about the two weeks we had planned, not two months, right when we are supposed to be launching a new STEM program for our youth, I would be leaping on you with gratitude."

"I expected you to leap regardless." His sexy grin did predictable things to her insides.

"You know two months is too long for me to take away from my job," she told him, needing her Sicilian tycoon lover to understand.

"I run a worldwide consortium and *I* am taking two months," he pointed out.

If that were true, she would feel very differently. Maybe.

"But you aren't taking two months off, are you? You have a state-of-the-art office on board that new yacht and you'll spend a few hours every day making sure that your family's multiple companies continue to run like clockwork."

His expression said he didn't get her point. "You require more sleep than I do, my few hours a day keeping my hand in will not impinge on our time together."

"I believe you'll do your best to make sure they don't, but I also know if an emergency arises, you'll deal with if it. Even if that means you calling in a helicopter to take you to be onsite."

"That happened once."

"During a date," she pointed out because the memory still rankled. He'd left her without a backward glance when they'd been very close to making love. "But in a space of two months, how many emergencies do you deal with?"

"We cannot foresee that."

"No, but we do *know* that my organization will have to hire a program coordinator to take my place, and there can be no guarantee they'll have a place for me when we return. Not to mention the fact that I will not have time to train my replacement how to get into the building, much less how to do the job, between now and our wedding." Which was only two days away. "And we also *know* that there will be lots of emergencies over the next two months getting that program up and running, but *I* won't be accessible to deal with them."

"You cannot compare your job to my role in Messina Shipping & Exports."

The company had started off as a humble exporter of olive oil and other agricultural goods from Sicily four generations in the past. Now it was one of the world's largest import-export brokers and had an entire fleet of cargo ships.

And even that hadn't been enough for her power broker fiancé. The tall, dark-haired Adonis had his own Venture Capitalist firm which had made him one of the richest men in Europe in his own right by the age of twenty-nine.

Not that any of that mattered to Annette. She'd fallen in love with Carlo the man, not Carlo the billionaire.

"No, and I've never tried to," she said now. "But I do ask that you respect that my job is very important *to me* even if it doesn't make me rich."

"You do not need to work once we are married," he said with arrogant assurance.

Pain filled her as she realized where this two-month long honeymoon was really coming from, and it wasn't her fiancé's desire to spend two months working parttime and remotely. He wanted her to quit her job. Had done since almost the moment she'd first taken it.

Only she thought they'd worked out that was not going to happen. "So, you've said."

She didn't understand his attitude. While his mother might not earn a salary for her volunteer work, the Sicilian socialite easily worked fulltime hours on her various charities and projects.

"Your job should not be more important than me." This time Carlo's frown was more of a scowl and she could see that something more than natural male arrogance was there, under the surface.

Only her own feelings of panic were taking precedence. This felt way too much like conversations she'd had with her father. Why must Annette choose to work in a career with no prestige? Didn't she see how her desire to work with at risk youth made their family look?

She thought it made them look like maybe they'd raised someone who cared about the world beyond her own front door. Her parents did not agree.

Social activism had its role, but not the one Annette wanted to take.

"No, of course not," she said responding to Carlo's words and not her father's playing over and over in her head. She wasn't putting the job ahead of him, but ahead of the luxury of a two-month-long honeymoon. "But how I feel about what I do *should* be important to you."

"You will find other worthy causes to support after we are married, *bèdda mia*."

"Like your mother?" she asked. Was the problem Annette earning an income?

"Perhaps not with the same level of time commitment."

Things started to become clearer in Annette's mind. She might be five years younger than him, but she was not ignorant. "You mean projects I can throw your money at, but not my time?" she asked with more anger than she'd realized she was holding.

His gorgeous grey eyes widened, like the anger in her tone surprised him too. "I am not being unreasonable."

"Telling me two days before the wedding that you want me to take practically the entire summer off from my position at a critical time for the program is more than unreasonable, it's selfish and manipulative. You don't want me to work and you're hoping that this will be the catalyst to force me into giving up my job."

She wanted him to deny the words so badly, her body ached with the tension it was holding.

"What if I am?" he demanded, slashing through the bubble of her dreams so they deflated too fast for even a pop of sound inside her heart. "I am a wealthy man, from an old family. Your job is an embarrassment to me."

She couldn't breathe for the pain in her chest.

His words were so like her father's they'd already been sharpened to such a fine point, they lacerated her heart with ease.

When she said nothing, he added. "We will be living in Sicily after the honeymoon, so you couldn't keep that job anyway."

And just like that, he dismissed her job as of no importance, telling Annette that the things closest to her heart didn't even register with the man she'd fallen in love with.

As a program coordinator for a social service organization, she could not be his perfect wife. But if she did not help others as she had always dreamed of doing, Annette could not, would not be herself.

So, that meant what? That he wanted to marry a different version of her, one that did not in fact exist. Annette had learned early and young that being something other than what was wanted, or expected, led to rejection and abandonment.

"When were you going to tell me that?" she asked painfully.

"I just did."

"But your office is in New York."

"My younger brother will be taking over the New York office. My father wants to retire and that means me taking over Messina Shipping & Exports."

"Your father wants to retire?" she asked, dumbfounded. Alceu Messina was an even bigger workaholic than his son.

"His doctor has told him he needs to minimize the stress in his life."

"Your father isn't well? Why didn't you tell me?" The feeling of being shielded from the truth did not wrap around her like a protective blanket, but upbraided her every exposed nerve ending.

She'd been left out of the loop with her own family too often to ever take it in stride from the man she intended to marry.

"He is not unwell, but he is ready to make a change in his life. He is sixty-seven after all, he has earned it."

"Yes, of course." Alceu and Valentina had their children later in life. Annette didn't know if that had been on purpose or because there had been complications. It wasn't something she and Carlo had ever talked about. Like too many things, it looked like.

"I still don't understand why you didn't tell me he wanted to retire."

"Papa doesn't want it getting out before I take over."

"But I'm not the media."

Carlo shrugged.

And so many things were becoming awfully, painfully clear she couldn't deal with the emotional fallout. "How long have you known?"

"Does it matter?"

"I think it does."

"He asked me to take over three months ago and we've been moving toward that transition since."

That explained why Carlo made so many extra trips to Sicily in the past months. "You didn't think I deserved to know *then* that you were going to move us to Europe?"

"I am telling you now."

"Why?"

"Don't be dense."

"I'm not being dense. I want to know why you didn't even talk to me before making that kind of monumental decision for both our lives."

"Why would I?"

And that, in a nutshell, said it all. Her opinions were unimportant. Her dreams were unimportant. Her desires were unimportant. They only mattered when they coincided with his.

Ultimately, *she* was unimportant.

She existed to him only as he wanted her to be, only he saw her as some construct he'd created in his own mind, not the woman she was. Could never be. Playing arm candy to a wealthy husband and socialite in training with his family was a role Annette was destined to fail at.

Just like she'd failed at being the kind of daughter her parents had wanted her to be.

She stared up at him, drinking in his gorgeous face, his muscular body, knowing she was likely seeing him for the last time. "You're so arrogant."

"You've said that before," he said with a slashing smile.

"But I'm not finding it charming right now. Your arrogance and selfishness are hurting me, and you don't even care." Could she get through to him?

Could she make him see that she was herself, not some version he'd concocted in his brain and Annette simply could not be anything other than *herself*?

"You will get over leaving your job," he said with absolute assurance.

"And leaving my sister? And the rest of my family," she tacked on, though Joyce was the only one Annette would actually miss.

Or who would miss her.

Their older sister had always resented the younger sibling who had been adopted when she was an only child. Their parents didn't even pretend anymore that they saw Annette the same way they did their two biological children.

But then, their reasons for adopting her had not been emotional, or even altruistic.

Carlo frowned. "You knew that one day we would have to move back to Sicily."

"One day in the future, not right now!"

"Now or then? What's the difference?"

She could see why he felt that way. For him, there was no difference. He'd never given any credence to her desire to do certain things with her organization before she left, how committed she was to starting a STEM program and building it into something she could be proud of. Something that would make a difference to children too often overlooked by the very agency created to serve them.

"It's always going to be like this with you, isn't it?" she asked as her heart cracked inside her chest.

"What do you mean?" He was starting to look just a tiny bit worried.

If business moguls ever actually worried about personal stuff, and she was not convinced they did.

"My feelings will always be secondary. The things I want, or need, out of life will always come down the priority list for you, if they make it on there at all."

"You want me. You need me. That is what is important."

"Not if it means losing *me*." She tugged the engagement ring off her finger.

The symbol she'd thought of love he could not express with words. It had been designed for her. Yellow gold with a beautiful floral design accented by diamonds and sapphires. Platinum was *de rigueur* in their set, but he'd had her ring made from her preferred precious metal. The floral design reflected her love of flowers and natural beauty.

He'd taken her desires into consideration when he'd had it made, why did they matter so little now?

"What are you doing?" he demanded.

She extended her hand with the ring in it toward him. "The wedding is off."

"Do not be melodramatic, *bèdda mia*. The wedding is not off. If it is that important to you, find a charity organization to support with your time once we return to Sicily after the wedding," he said, like making a hugely magnanimous gesture. "Parttime of course."

"Your mother easily works fulltime."

"I know."

And once again in a matter of minutes, lightbulbs went on in her brain, illuminating truths Annette had overlooked during their time together.

What she had always seen as a point of concurrence for them, was in fact a wedge that would drive them apart. "How did I never realize you resented your mother's time on her work?"

"I never said I did." But his expression? That closed off, emotionless mask said it all.

Something about Valentina's commitment to her various causes had hurt Carlo, leaving him with the certainty that *his* wife should put their family first.

And Annette had never even realized that was an issue. How unseeing had she been? So wrapped up in her own glowing version of their relationship she'd ignored every indicator that their views of the world did not mesh.

"This," Annette indicated him and her with a gesture of her hand. "It says it loud and clear."

"I want our children to have your attention."

"We aren't having children right away," she said with exasperation. They'd discussed it and agreed to wait at least a couple of years. She was leaning more toward five or six.

She was marrying young because she'd fallen in love, that didn't mean she wanted everything else happening at a pace.

"My father wants to meet his grandchildren before he dies."

"His health is that serious?" she asked, her heart squeezing in her chest. She *liked* Alceu, though he was every bit as much of a workaholic as his sons had been raised to be.

"No. As I said, he is not ill, but he is nearing seventy."

And would probably live to see ninety at least.

"Yet another decision you planned to make without me?" she asked, her tone harsh.

She'd spent years working so hard to earn her family's love, being placid when inside she was roiling with anger sometimes, pursuing activities she didn't enjoy in the least to please adopted parents that never seemed to think she measured up.

Annette had promised herself she wouldn't marry a man who expected the same from her. She'd thought she'd found him.

She'd been spectacularly wrong.

"I could hardly do that, could I?" he asked, this time annoyance and impatience loud and clear in his tone.

He referred, of course, to the fact that she had opted to use an IUD for birth control, once they had become physically intimate. It was only coming out on her say so. She was talking about something far more important than the mechanics of birth control. Annette was referring to sharing decisions as equals, to respecting one another's goals and dreams.

She didn't have to run a multinational corporation for the time she spent at work to have value. No, she didn't employ thousands of people, but she made a difference in the lives of the youth she served.

Apparently, he did not see things the same way.

At all.

"I cannot marry you," she said again, each word a slashing wound to her heart. Annette tried to hand him the ring again. "I'm not the right woman for you."

"I will be the judge of that, *caro*." Carlo looked at her with indulgence rather than anger, and totally ignored her outstretched hand. "Of course, you can marry me. Things may be happening more quickly than either of us expected in certain regards, but it is nothing to fear."

She wasn't afraid of being a mother, but neither was she ready for that role just yet. "You expect me to jettison my job and move to Sicily."

"You knew we would have to move there at some point, that you could not stay with your organization long term."

"Yes, but I had plans, goals for what I could do while I was there."

"So, make new plans. Set new goals." His tone implied this was not rocket science.

"If I married you, it would always be like this, wouldn't it? Me changing to fit your plans, you making decisions without my input."

He sighed. "Perhaps, I should have spoken to you about the move, but *cara*, you must understand, the last weeks have been intense. It took a great deal to clear my schedule for the honeymoon. My father's decision to retire came unexpectedly, even for me."

A two-month-long honeymoon she had not asked for and did not want. Not to mention emotionally painful and stressful, not that Carlo would admit to anything that might resemble weakness.

"He works too many hours and dines on stress," Annette said, realizing she might as well be describing Carlo. She still found it hard to believe Alceu wanted to retire.

His health *must* be more precarious than Carlo was acknowledging. But was that because Carlo refused to see it, or he simply didn't want to share it with her?

Her Sicilian lover shrugged. "He will have to learn to eat food instead," he joked.

"Yes, but it's not your father that's worrying me." She sighed, realizing how callous that sounded. "I don't mean I don't care about him. I do care. Very much, but he's not the problem."

"No, your job is the problem."

She shook her head. "It's not my job. It's me. You want me to be something I'm not, someone I'm not even sure I could ever be, even if I was willing to try."

"You are talking nonsense. Listen, this is just prewedding jitters. You will feel better after we are wed."

"I am not going to marry you." She held the ring out again, pain so heavy she wasn't sure she could hold it inside. "Take it. I mean it, Carlo."

But he remained with his hands stubbornly down. "I will not. I will be standing at the front of the church waiting for you in two days' time. I expect you to be there. Whatever problems you think we have, we can work them out later. We have a lifetime."

He turned and strode away without another word.

Annette tried to shout after him, but she could not make the words come.

No matter what he thought, that was not how it worked. Whatever problems they had would follow them into marriage. And this problem was insurmountable.

She was not the right woman for him.

And as much as it hurt to admit, *he was not the right man for her.*

One thing she knew with absolute certainty, being alone was better than living with someone who needed her to be something other than her authentic self to accept her. She'd lived that way since she was five years old, until she'd gone away to university.

She could not live that way again.

Not ever.

Chapter Six

Chapter 6

Annette came out of her fugue of memories to note her sister had left the terrace and she was entirely alone. It was not a new feeling.

She'd basically been alone since becoming the unwanted baggage from her birth father's first marriage, dumped with his brother to appease his new wife. Named Annette after her mother, Anne, her adoptive family had instantly started calling her Netta in deference to the woman now married to William Hudson. Apparently, Annette looked too much like her birth mother as well, serving as a continual reminder of a past both her birth father and his second wife would prefer to forget.

She was blonde and blue eyed, like her deceased mother. Everyone else in the Hudson clan were brunettes. Kimber, the woman who her birth father had married, was even a brunette, though she had salon perfected red highlights. At five-feet-three inches, Annette was shorter than all the other women in her family too. Where they were tall and svelte, she was short and curvy.

Unlike her sisters, she could never wear a garment straight off the runway.

Carlo hadn't seemed to mind though. He'd called her his pocket Venus and complimented her blue eyes, often saying they glowed like sapphires. When they'd had sex after her sister's wedding, he'd said he liked her natural blonde hair better than the lowlights too.

If only his appreciation for her body translated to him caring about and approving of the person she was. It didn't though.

And now she understood better where five years of silence had come from.

He had truly believed she would show up at the church. He'd trusted her to keep her promise to marry him and because she'd left telling people the wedding was off to her parents, no one had disabused him of that notion.

She'd literally left him standing at the altar and all her reasons for her behavior five years ago didn't change that. Not for the first time, she realized she owed him an apology. One without qualifiers or explanations.

She thought he should be sorry too, for the high-handed way he'd tried to dictate her life five years ago. However, if therapy had taught her anything, it was that Annette could not dictate the actions of others. She only had agency over her own, but she did have that agency and had to always remember that.

Needing to make sure things were okay between her and Joyce, or simply looking for a way to put off the upcoming discussion with Carlo, Annette went back inside the villa.

She found her sister sitting between their mother and their oldest sister, Lynette.

The look she gave Annette indicated that had not been happenstance on her part. Joyce didn't want another private tete-e-tete with Annette and she'd chosen the perfect avoidance.

Hurt, but unwilling to approach her younger sister when she'd placed herself between allies so hostile to Annette, she looked around the large drawing room for sign of either the baby, or Carlo.

She found them together with Fantino. Carlo was holding Jocinda oh so carefully, his expression one of wonder and unabashed affection as he looked down at the tiny infant.

Fantino was talking about some business deal and for once it was clear he only had half his brother's attention on the company matter. The way the young father kept reaching out to run a finger down his daughter's soft cheek, or touch her little foot showed that maybe his attention wasn't fully focused on what he was saying either.

The younger Messina looked up as Annette approached. "Ah, Annette. Joyce was hoping the two of you could spend some time together alone."

Not anymore, she wasn't. But Annette didn't say that. She simply gave Fantino what she thought of as her *family* smile, the one that hid all real emotion. "That would be nice. I wouldn't mind some time with this beautiful little girl, either."

Carlo's head snapped up, like he'd just now realized Annette was there. For one second his grey gaze flashed with welcome and the heat that was always there, under the surface, between them. Then his face shuttered, and he looked to his brother. "Set up the meeting. I'll have my team put together the numbers and proposal you and I have discussed."

So much for him only listening with partial attention. She should have known better. Nothing got between Carlo and business. Not even their adorable new baby niece.

"Bonu," Fantino said. "I appreciate—"

Carlo interrupted his brother's thanks, saying something like no problem, that's what brothers are for in Sicilian. Close enough to Italian, which she spoke fluently, for her to understand, Annette still wouldn't have tried to speak the native dialect of Sicily.

"May I hold her?" Annette asked Fantino, indicating Jocinda.

"If you can prise her away from my brother." Fantino laughed at his own joke, though Annette still thought he looked exhausted.

"Jocinda isn't sleeping through the night?" she asked.

She'd thought the baby was because of something Joyce had said on one of their video calls, but neither parent was rested enough for that to be true.

Something skittered across the younger brother's features, but he shrugged. "Jet lag."

Funny, she didn't believe him when he said it any more than she'd believed herself using the excuse earlier. "If I can help in any way..." She let her voice trail off, worried Fantino would throw her offer back in her face as Joyce had done.

He didn't, but his shrug said it all. How could she help?

"Tonight. I can stay with her and get up with her so you and Joyce can sleep the night through."

"Oh, would you?" The abject relief on Fantino's face was hard to bear.

"Why haven't you hired a nanny, or something?" she asked.

Fantino and Carlo shared a significant look. "Joyce and I are raising our daughter, not a nanny," Fantino said, sounding defensive.

Annette had no desire to push it and perhaps have him back out on letting her stay with the baby that night. If she could give her sister and brother-in-law a night of uninterrupted rest, she was going to.

"It sounds like you'll have plenty of time holding little Jocinda tonight," Carlo said smugly. "She is content with me right now."

"Until your phone rings," Annette teased.

Carlo shook his head. "You are feeling very brave when I have a baby in my arms."

"I don't remember Annette ever hesitating to tease you before," Fantino offered with a tired smile.

"Why Jocinda?" Carlo asked, ignoring his brother's comment. "Mama and Papa were wondering as well. It is not a family name on either side."

"Isn't it?" Fantino asked, his tone implying he thought Carlo should know the answer to his own question.

"I have never heard it used."

"Do you have to use family names for your children?" Annette asked lightly. "Surely, that would get confusing."

"No, of course not. We Messinas are not that hidebound," Carlo said.

"Well, then..." Annette didn't know why, but she was loathe to be there when someone explained to Carlo that his baby niece had been named for her, and not just her, but the nickname that had played so heavily in the scandal that followed their breakup.

Cinderella.

All discussion was abandoned when Valentina arrived on the scene, insistent on holding her first grandchild. "Your father and I are keeping the baby tonight, so you and dear Joyce can sleep through."

"I already offered," Annette said when Fantino just stared at his mother, like he was trying to parse her words.

"Nonsense," Valentina said with finality. "You are young. Go out, enjoy yourself tonight. I am sure my son can be prevailed upon to accompany you."

"Fantino?" Annette asked senselessly.

But Valentina couldn't possibly mean Carlo, could she? And she didn't have any other sons.

Valentina's laugh startled the baby, who was quickly settled, but not before Joyce arrived looking harried. "Is she alright?"

"She is fine, *cara*. Do not worry. Her grandmother has her."

Both Messina men stared at their mother like the sight of her with a babe in her arms was entirely unexpected.

Annette rolled her eyes. "She had you both, if you will remember."

But the two brothers just shrugged. Like that didn't signify.

Valentina cooed down at the baby, ignoring her sons. Or so Annette thought.

"The boys think because I left certain care to their nannies and grandmother that I do not know how to care for a baby, I suppose. My causes kept me from them too often, but just as Alceu has had to slow down, so have I. I have every intention of spending lots of quality time with my first grandchild."

The look on Carlo's face was a cross between shock and pain.

And another thing about this man slotted into place. Valentina had been an absentee mother and Annette already knew their father had been a workaholic. So, that left their grandmother and the nannies.

Annette finally understood why his mother's volunteerism was not a source of pride so much as pain for Carlo, and clearly Fantino as well.

What she did not understand was why they didn't seem to blame their father for being equally, if not more absent from their formative years?

Annette would never question the power of Valentina's will again. Not when she sat in the passenger seat of Carlo's sleek black sports car.

"You'll be 35 this year, don't you think it's time for a more sedate form of transportation?" she joked as the scent of the leather upholstery teased her senses.

"Don't you know that 35 is when most men buy their first sportscar?" he bantered back.

"Not the men I know." But then the men she knew were her father, who had a luxury sedan and the requisite driver to go with it, and the men associated with her nonprofit organization.

The latter drove electric cars, sometimes hybrids, and none of them still had the new car smell clinging to them.

"Let me guess, your dates drive sedate fuel-efficient compacts."

"If we're going to save the planet, somebody has to." She didn't launch into her usual speech about the *reduce* part of the reduce, reuse and recycle motto.

For one thing, Carlo had heard it all before.

For another, she was enjoying the ride in the luxury sports car too much to say anything without feeling like a hypocrite. She also didn't mention that she didn't date. That was a little tidbit Annette thought she'd rather keep to herself.

They were sharing a lovely meal at a tiny restaurant that catered to the wealthy locals. No tourists here. Very few guests at all and a menu fixed by the chef that changed nightly based on local produce.

Annette was enchanted and said so.

"It is one of my favorite places to eat. Other places, it can be difficult for security to keep people who want to meet a Messina away from the table."

She knew he spoke the truth. While Carlo and his family would move countries before being in a reality television show, they were as well known in Sicily as the Kardashians were in America.

Security was such a natural part of the billionaire's lifestyle, Annette hadn't really paid attention when a car kept pace with theirs on the drive to the restaurant. Or when one of the men from it had taken up an inobtrusive position on the periphery of the establishment. He wasn't the only security man watching over a client here, but the restaurant had been designed to give the illusion of privacy, if not the reality.

"I owe you an apology," she said after the wine had been tested and poured.

Carlo jerked his head in the negative. "I did not want to talk about it five years ago, and I do not wish to discuss it now."

"But I am sorry. Please believe me, Carlo. If I had it to do over again, I would have done things differently."

"If *differently* doesn't include showing up at the church, prepared to speak your vows, I'm not interested."

"You have a very binary view of the world, did you know that?"

"In some things, like keeping one's promises? Yes, I suppose I do."

She stifled a sigh. "I never meant to hurt you."

"I never said you hurt me, but you did humiliate me. The media vultures were just a small part of it."

"I know. I'm sor—"

"Do not say it again. We start afresh. Now. You are the sister of my sister-in-law. The aunt and godmother to my very precious niece. Our history is no longer what is important, but our family's future."

"I agree, but—"

"No buts. This is the way it has to be, Annette."

Hearing him call her by name hurt in a way all its own, she realized. He'd always used to call her his beauty, or darling. He'd only used her name when they were making love and it had felt special then.

Now it felt like another barrier between them.

Despite the barriers, Annette had a wonderful time with Carlo. So long as she kept the conversation well away from their shared past, he was an interested and interesting companion.

He took her dancing and somehow, they found themselves on the dance floor for all the slower songs. Carlo held her close, sometimes singing along to the song lyrics in a surprisingly fine baritone.

As the night wore on, Annette's defenses against his sensual pull crumbled bit by bit.

Because he treated her like a date, not a woman he despised and could not trust.

When he took her to a hotel after dancing, she did not demur. Once again, Annette was making her own choices and she chose to spend the night in Carlo's arms.

This time she was fully aware she would not wake up with him beside her.

Their lovemaking was every bit as frenzied as after her sister's wedding. Only this time, it felt like a beginning, not an ending.

Which is what she'd told herself the last time, so she could hardly trust it.

However, Carlo was there the next morning when she woke. Working, yes, but still in the hotel suite. He'd ordered her breakfast again, but this time it was her favorite crepes and cups of the freshly brewed Sicilian coffee she adored.

Annette took her time over breakfast, noticing quickly that again, Carlo was very intent on steering the conversation in decidedly non-personal channels. He even told her about his latest deal, for goodness's sake.

She listened raptly though, interested despite herself.

He asked about her work and Annette found herself telling him about what she'd learned about hiring and salary practices at her organization.

Instead of dismissing her concerns to naivete, Carlo listened and offered his attorneys to help her set things right if she needed. "Even if you don't want to pull that trigger, you can text me any time for advice."

Overcome, Annette swallowed back emotion she knew he didn't want to deal with. "Thank you."

They made love again but took post coital showers separately by silent agreement. She wanted to get back to the villa and see her sister. He had work to do. The fact he'd stayed so late with her on a Monday sent warm fuzzies fizzing through her like just uncorked champagne.

However, when they got back to the villa later, it was to find Valentina in a state. Joyce had insisted on returning home early. She, Fantino and Jocinda had left for the airport right after breakfast. Since they were flying in the company jet, they only had to wait for a takeoff slot, not a scheduled flight.

And the Sicilian airport wasn't nearly as busy as the one in Rome.

Chapter Seven

As worried as she was for her sister, Annette couldn't help enjoying her time with Carlo. She spent her last day and a half with his parents during business hours and with Carlo after. He worked his schedule so he got off much earlier than usual both days and they visited sites in Sicily she'd yet to see.

As wonderful as their time together was, Annette was very aware how Carlo never wanted to discuss the past or any prospect of a future.

When it came time for her to go to the airport, his father drove her because Carlo had a business call he had to take.

"I could have caught a taxi," Annette said, pretty sure it was true. "Or simply ridden with one of your security people. You didn't have to go out of your way."

As she said the words, she realized how much she wished that Carlo had gone out of his though. But the last three days had been a sexual tryst, nothing else, and if she let herself forget that, she was in for a world of hurt.

"Nonsense, you are family."

Unable to deny that assertion, Annette simply said, "Well, thank you."

When her brother-in-law called two weeks later and asked her to come, Annette was worried, but not surprised. She'd only had one video chat with Joyce since returning from Europe and her sister had swung between snappish and apathetic with erratic frequency.

Annette had already arranged to step down from her new job, and to take a sabbatical from the company. She'd begun packing to move back to New York, so it was simply a matter of getting a storage container and asking her coworkers to come by and help her fill it. Her things would be shipped to New York and stored at a facility until she'd found a place to live.

Although she and Carlo had been texting even more regularly than before, Annette didn't tell him of her plans to move. He was still in Sicily, so Portland or New York made little difference to him, she was sure.

They'd tried sexting, but both had found it far more hilarious than sexy, and they'd advanced to video chats for their *booty calls*. There could be no question that their relationship was mainly about sex, so Annette didn't tell Carlo about Fantino's call either, or her plans for the present to stay with her sister's family and help however she could.

When Joyce called Annette after the Messina jet landed in the small Upstate New York airport, the younger woman was sobbing and begging her sister to come. Annette had never been so grateful for timing in her life, because she was already in the car Fantino had had waiting for her and on her way to their home.

When she arrived, Joyce was in no better state than she'd been on the phone and Fantino looked wrung out, though he was admitting no weakness.

Typical Messina man.

The first week flew by as Annette did her best to take care of Jo-Jo without help. Fantino spent the weekdays in the city and while he did his best to care for his daughter on the weekends, he also had an emotionally fragile wife to contend with.

Annette never knew if she was going to be dealing with weepy Joyce, angry Joyce, or lost and confused Joyce from one minute to the next. She did her best to shield the baby from the tension that laid a pall over the adults in the beautiful Upstate New York mansion, while struggling with unexpected exhaustion.

Taking care of an infant who did not sleep through the night by any stretch was far more taxing than she'd expected. Annette could not nap while Jo-Jo did during the day, because then she was busy with her sister. Joyce had confided to Annette only yesterday that she'd had thoughts of harming herself and the baby.

Annette was trying to convince both Joyce and Fantino that the new mom needed professional help. Until then, she was doing her best, with the help of the mansion's staff, to make sure that neither the baby, nor Joyce, were left alone. The stress was taking its toll and Annette felt constantly nauseated and tired.

She still hadn't talked to Carlo about the move, but she planned to change that tonight. They had a video chat scheduled, but instead of having cybersex, they were going to talk.

Joyce had Fantino's promise that he would stay with his wife and not disappear into his study for work, after dinner. Annette had a baby monitor set up in Jo-Jo's room, so she could hear if the baby cried. With her preparations in place, she shut the door to her room and got comfy in an armchair by the window, tucking her feet under her.

Her guestroom was on the west side, and if it had been earlier, she would have had a gorgeous view of the sunset as she sipped a cup of herbal tea and waited for Carlo's call. As it was, she stared out into the inky blackness of a winter night too cloudy for stars.

When her phone buzzed, she swiped to answer, the video taking a moment longer to connect than a voice call.

From the angle, it was obvious Carlo had his phone in a stand that would allow him hands free movement, but she held hers close so her face took up most of the screen. "Hi, Carlo."

"*Bèdda mia*, it is good to see you."

"It's good to see you too." She realized how true the words were as she said them.

Just seeing Carlo's capable and handsome face on her phone screen gave her a sense of calm that had been missing for the past week. She wasn't alone. He would have an idea of what to do, how to convince both Joyce and Fantino to get Joyce help.

Both were equally intransigent about therapy and the need for it.

That was for other people. Joyce could sort her own problems. Or so they assured Annette. The fact Annette had spent three years in therapy after moving to Portland was seen as unfortunate, not the shining example of rational behavior she'd hoped they might acknowledge it.

Joyce simply said she thought her sister should be able to help her then.

Neither wanted to admit that Joyce was suffering any sort of depression. And Annette was no professional. Despite all the training she'd taken to work with at risk youth, Annette wasn't about to diagnose her sister with postpartum depression, but she desperately wanted Joyce to see someone who could determine if that was the cause of her sister's doldrums and frightening thoughts.

"You look contemplative," Carlo said.

"I am." She sighed. "We need to talk about Joyce and Fantino."

He frowned, his body tensing. "No."

"What do you mean, no? I need your advice." Maybe even his help. He could talk to Fantino, couldn't he?

Tell his younger brother that there was nothing wrong with seeking psychological support for Joyce.

"My advice is to stay out of your sister's marriage."

"Carlo, you don't know—"

"No. Listen to yourself, Annette. You did not want to marry and have a family. That does not mean it was a bad choice for Joyce."

"It hasn't turned out to be all sunshine and roses for her either," Annette insisted.

"Who said it would? Or even should be? Life is not always easy, but she and Fantino must work through their own problems."

"Have you been talking to Fantino?" she asked suspiciously. Was *Carlo* the reason the younger Messina brother was so anti-therapy?

"I talk to my brother frequently."

So, he knew about what was happening and he thought she should butt out? Like her mom and dad did.

"Look, sometimes people need professional help dealing with their problems."

"Fantino and Joyce do not have those sorts of problems."

"You are not serious."

"Listen to me, Annette. You need to let Joyce find her happiness."

"That's what I'm talking about."

"By driving a wedge between her and Fantino? By filling her head with ideas of starting a career when she's still settling into new motherhood?"

"What are you talking about? Though if getting a job would help her, I'm all for it. It's her choice, Carlo."

"Exactly. Not mine. Not *yours*."

"You act like I have some kind of agenda here."

"Don't you?"

"Only to help my sister get better."

"Regularly sleeping through the night will help more than any sisterly advice, I am sure."

Exhausted and on edge herself, Annette was in no mood to deal with Carlo's opinions on that score. She was the one losing sleep so her sister could get some. After a week, Joyce didn't show any improvement from it.

"When your father asked me to talk to you and suggest you let your sister find her feet in her new marriage and motherhood, I told him I didn't think it was necessary, but I can see I was wrong."

"You've been speaking to my father?"

"We talk regularly. We share common business interests, you remember."

"I am not a business interest!" She was losing her cool and that was not okay, but Carlo and her father?

Annette could just imagine what had been said about her and none of it good.

"No, but as his daughter, you are a concern."

"You know what? Never mind. If you and my father have the same view of the situation, you're not going to help me." Once again, the weight of being on her own pressed down her.

"Gladly. I did not call you to talk about our siblings." He gave her that slashing smile that usually sent her nerve endings zinging.

Tonight, all it did was make her want to cry.

Because that smile in that moment might as well have been a meteorite hitting her world. It told her that their relationship wasn't just mostly about sex, but it was all about sex. She was an easy booty call. He didn't even have to leave his apartment, because here she was on the other end of a video call.

And if Annette was wired for easy, casual sex, that would be fine.

She wasn't. No matter what she tried to tell herself. And this pseudo friendship that wasn't really a friendship at all wasn't enough of a relationship to make the sex okay with her brain, much less her heart.

"I need to go."

"You look tired. Get some sleep. We'll set something up for later in the week."

Yeah, no. She just shook her head and signed off the video call.

Joyce's voice risen to the point of screaming had her running from her room in search of her sister. She found her in the living room, sobbing on the floor in front of a large ornate mirror, now broken like someone had thrown something at it.

The culprit, a small statue that used to sit on the mantle lay on the carpet below.

Fantino was trying to comfort his wife. Between the two of them, he and Annette finally got Joyce up to their bedroom and into a soothing bath.

"You are right. She needs help that you and I cannot give her." Fantino sounded so sad, but also determined.

It took another month, with more incidents just like that one, before he and Joyce took the Messina jet to California to check her into a private clinic. Joyce had insisted on Southern California because she'd wanted away from New York's cold winter.

Annette was just glad her sister was willing to get help. She deserved to be happy.

Annette sat in numb silence, waiting for the lawyer to speak. She didn't understand why she had to be here for this. Surely Carlo could handle the business stuff. She didn't understand why everyone else was there as well, a living will wasn't like a regular will, was it?

But everyone was there. Her parents, Lynette, Carlo and his parents.

No Joyce or Fantino though. They were the reason everyone had been called to the lawyer's office. Annette's baby sister was in a coma along with her husband. A semi-truck driven by a man who'd had too little sleep on roads slick with ice had crossed three lanes to run into their car as they returned from the airport. Annette shook her head, unable to believe what was happening.

Joyce had worked hard at regaining her equilibrium at the clinic. Their last video chat before she and Fantino returned to New York had shown the sister Annette remembered, a vibrant woman who couldn't wait to see her baby in person.

Now, she hovered in a no man's land between life and death, her injuries so severe, she could die before she ever woke up.

With both her parents in comas none of the doctors could be sure they would ever come out of, Jo-Jo was as much an orphan as Annette had ever been. She was determined her niece would never feel the pain of not being wanted as she had. Annette would take care of Jo-Jo, making sure the baby knew she was absolutely loved and wanted.

Annette's numbness turned to horror as she heard the terms of her sister's and then her brother-in-law's respective living wills. In the unlikely event that both were incapacitated for any length of time, they had placed Jo-Jo under the sole guardianship of Carlo.

"But that can't be right!"

The lawyer stopped speaking and gave her a censorious glance. "If I could continue?"

What else was there to say? What else mattered? "But he barely knows Jo-Jo."

He'd met the baby when she was born and then seen her again at the christening. It was the only time he'd held the baby that she knew of. Yes, Carlo had been good with her, but he hadn't been to New York to see his niece in the intervening months. And now they were saying Carlo was to be the baby's guardian?

"For the past three months I'm the one who has fed Jo-Jo, woken in the middle of the night to comfort her, played with her, bathed her, changed all her diapers." Joyce has spent six weeks at the clinic. Fantino had been there for the first two and then on the weekends thereafter.

One thing neither one had moved on though was their unwillingness to hire a nanny, so Annette had been on her own taking care of Jo-Jo. Not that she'd ever really considered herself on her own with a house full of staff.

"Perhaps pushing your way in where you don't belong is why your sister had such a hard time coming to grips with motherhood," Elise Hudson said with angry judgment.

Old pain from her adopted mother's many rejections pricked at Annette's soul.

"You know that's not true," Annette said softly, her voice cracked with emotion. "I only stepped in when Fantino asked me to help, when it was obvious Joyce wasn't coping."

"So you claim. However, both your sister and her husband have made it crystal clear who they wished to take guardianship of the child," Annette's father said coldly. "And it wasn't you. I'm sure we all have no difficulty understanding why."

"I don't understand why." Despair and desperation became a tight vice around Annette's heart. She owed her sister. She owed Jo-Jo.

Annette had to take care of the baby until her own parents were capable of doing so. She refused to believe they wouldn't come out of their comas.

Carlo just sat there in silence, his expression unreadable.

"If you need help securing a flight back to Portland, my administrative assistant will see to it." That was Carlo, finally putting his oar in.

This was him getting back at her for ignoring his texts and other attempts to get in touch over the past couple of months. Annette simply hadn't had the wherewithal to deal with her complicated feelings where Carlo was concerned. She'd accepted he only wanted sex and she had admitted to herself that she needed more.

So, she'd ghosted him. Fair? Maybe not, but Annette had spent a good part of those months exhausted herself, finally adjusting to her new sleep schedule just this past week.

She'd thought it was a sign. Everything was getting better. That incessant stress nausea had finally settled down too.

"I don't care what those papers say, I'm not going anywhere until Joyce and Fantino are well enough to care for their child." Annette tried to sound firm, but her voice broke at the last.

Joyce and Fantino had to get better. They just had to.

Chapter Eight

Carlo frowned. "Pamina will be with Jocinda. You do not need to worry about her safety and well-being."

"Pamina? You're trusting her care to a woman who has known Jo-Jo less than a week?"

"Pamina is her nanny, naturally I trust her to care for our niece." He looked pained, like explaining himself was far from what he wanted to be doing. "She came with the highest of recommendations from a reputable agency."

Who cared? Pamina was not Annette. "Jo-Jo needs *family*." The baby needed *her*.

Annette was the only consistent in the baby's life right now. None of the rest of the family, on either side, had enough of a bond with Jo-Jo to take over for Annette. As much as it hurt Annette to acknowledge, Jo-Jo did not cry for her parents when she was distressed now. She wanted Annette.

Annette had offered to come with them to California and bring Jo-Jo, but Joyce had been adamantly opposed to the idea. They'd learned that was part of what turned out to be a pretty severe case of postpartum depression. Joyce had not bonded with her daughter because she'd been emotionally unavailable. She'd wanted to change that as soon as they got back to New York. It was Annette's job to make sure Jo-Jo felt loved and secure until that could happen.

Once her sister and Fantino were well. They *would* get well.

And nanny, or no nanny, Annette wasn't going anywhere until Joyce and Fantino had come home. Ridiculously duped, she'd believed Pamina was Carlo's clumsy attempt at giving *her* support after the accident. Valentina and Alceu had gone straight to the hospital, dropping in twice to see how she was doing and murmuring their approval upon finding a nanny in residence to help her.

Carlo had not been to the house in the week since the tragedy, not that Annette blamed him. His brother had been in ICU that entire time. What time he wasn't spending overseeing the company and covering for his brother, he'd been at the hospital.

While Annette had longed to be there as well, at her sister's bedside, she'd only been able to visit once because she had to do what was best for Jo-Jo.

The nanny had taken direction easily from Annette and had never once alluded to the fact that Carlo was her employer, not Annette. She'd seen the bond Annette had with Jo-Jo and remarked upon it with approval, expressing relief the baby had someone consistent in her life.

Annette had liked Pamina and considered her a godsend.

"How can a workaholic like you take care of a baby?" she demanded. "You've been her effective parent for a week and you knew that, but you haven't made the time to even check in on her once!"

"I speak to Pamina daily."

"She never told me that." And it did not help Annette's feelings. Because how involved could those discussions have been if the fact Annette was there had never come up? "Anyway, it's not the same as being there. What if Jo-Jo didn't like her?"

"My parents assured me that Jocinda and Pamina were a good fit."

But clearly they hadn't mentioned that Annette had been there, taking care of the baby already. Did no one in her life think she was worthy of being family, much less even mentioned?

Jo-Jo needed her. Couldn't they all see that? She looked wildly around the office filled with people Annette couldn't help feeling despised her, regardless of anything said in the past.

Valentina was looking at her with pity. Alceu wasn't looking at her at all. He seemed entirely checked out of the proceedings, grey with stress that only seemed to grow the longer his son stayed in a coma.

Annette's parents were looking at her all right and their expressions were not warm.

"If you'd left well enough alone, Joyce would have stepped up and been the mother she needed to be," her mother accused. "They would never have been in California in the first place."

Those words hit Annette like a body blow and she stumbled. "No," she whispered. "Don't say that."

"Jocinda is better off without you in her life, just as your sister would have been," her mother went on remorselessly.

"That is enough." Carlo's words came out like bullets. "Annette did not cause the crash."

"We are all upset," Valentina added. "However, blaming one another will do nothing to bring either of our children out of coma any faster."

Elise pressed her lips together tightly, saying nothing more, but the look she gave Annette was filled with condemnation.

Guilt beat at Annette because she knew her mother was right about one thing. Jo-Jo's parents would not be in hospital if they had not gone to the clinic in California for treatment.

"She needed help," Annette said to no one in particular. "Joyce was suffering from a hormone and chemical imbalance." Her sister had continued to have thoughts of self-harm and hurting Jo-Jo, even when Annette was there taking care of them both. "It wasn't going to get better on its own."

"Back in my day, a woman knew she had to do whatever it took to be a mother. My daughter would have gotten over her *hormones* if you hadn't interfered," Elise said staunchly.

"I'm your daughter too," Annette couldn't help saying. She might be adopted, but she was still *theirs*. Hadn't they all said it often enough?

Her dad wasn't her daddy anymore. Now that was Floyd Hudson, not his brother William. She'd been punished every time she'd forgotten that important fact and called the wrong man dad.

"No daughter of ours would make the kinds of choices you've made with your life." Her father's expression was every bit as repudiating as his tone.

One might think he had never forgiven her for calling off the wedding, but really her father had never actually forgiven Annette for catching Carlo's eye in the first place. He'd wanted the billionaire businessman for Lynette.

Annette cracked right down the center of her soul. These were her parents and they wouldn't help her.

No one was going to help her and she wasn't going to be allowed to help Jo-Jo.

The room pressed in on Annette, pain and fear making her heart ache in her chest, her breath come in unsatisfying pants. Lightheaded, she stumbled back to her chair, only vaguely aware of a strong, guiding hand.

"Sit. Let the lawyer finish and then we will speak." That was Carlo's voice, sounding kind.

Annette nodded, but did not speak.

The lawyer continued, his voice an indistinct drone going on about financial details she paid no attention to. All Annette could think was how to convince Carlo to let Annette remain in Jo-Jo's life until Joyce woke up from her coma.

Her whirling thoughts were not coming up with anything though, and her desperation and sadness grew.

"Here, drink this." A cup of coffee hovered in front of Annette's gaze, its scent bringing her out of the morass in her head.

The strong olive toned hand holding it was steady. Annette's gaze flicked up to Carlo. His face was set in stoic lines, his body language giving away nothing of how he was feeling.

"Carlo, please. Don't take Jo-Jo away from me," she begged.

"Drink your coffee."

The smell of coffee mixed with brandy wafted toward her and she shook her head. "No. No brandy. I have to be able to think."

"To do what? You aren't going back to the mansion tonight."

She had planned to do that, but now she thought the next day would be better spent consulting an attorney. "I'm going to fight the guardianship assignment." Though she had no idea how.

He shook his head.

But she was determined. "I have to protect Jo-Jo."

"You don't have to protect our niece from me."

"Not from you, but from the pain of neglect, of being unwanted? Yes, I do!" But that had been her, not Jo-Jo. Annette had been neglected and unwanted.

Even if he was a workaholic, Carlo loved their niece.

"You are being irrational. Have you even slept since getting the news?" He put the coffee down on the low table beside her chair. Had it been there before? She couldn't remember.

Annette looked around the lawyer's office, meeting room, whatever...and realized it was empty. Her family were gone and so was his. So was the lawyer and his paralegal.

"Where is everyone?" she asked.

"All the necessary legal matters have been seen to. They left."

"Jo-Jo is the only thing that matters as far as I'm concerned."

"I think you would find it difficult to take care of her without a place to live," he said prosaically. "You cannot think to take our niece back to Portland with you."

"I can stay in Joyce and Fantino's home. They'll return to it." She felt compelled to add, "Eventually."

Because even if her sister and/or brother-in-law woke up today, they both had healing to do before leaving the hospital. Their injuries had been severe, though Joyce's most serious injury was the head trauma that had put her in a coma. She had numerous lacerations that had required stitches. With a broken leg and shoulder, Fantino would need physical therapy as well.

"And pay the staff with what? Buy groceries and pay the not insignificant utilities with what exactly?"

"I have some money set by." She moved restlessly. "What does any of that matter? Jo-Jo needs me."

"You keep saying that."

"Because it is true!"

He nodded. "I am willing to concede the point, though I have always been told that babies are resilient. One way, or another, Jocinda will be fine."

"Stop calling her that! Fantino and Joyce called her Jo-Jo. She deserves to be called by the name her parents gave her."

"They named her Jocinda."

"After me and Joyce. Doesn't that tell you anything?"

"Your name is not Cindy."

"Joyce thought it was funny to call me Cinderella. She didn't find the stories in the media the tragedy everyone else did, but laughed at them." And her baby sister had said the name fit too well, the way Annette had always served her family.

Carlo didn't look like he believed her.

"When have I ever lied to you?"

"When you promised to marry me."

"Get over it!" For once the guilt of jilting him was not paramount. "Relationships end. You can't let your personal feelings toward me hurt Jo-Jo. You're responsible for her now." At least until Joyce and Fantino could take back the responsibility.

"I am aware." Carlo's tone and expression said he realized how serious that commitment was and maybe it wasn't one he'd been looking for.

"You need to listen to me, Carlo."

"I have listened to you, but I also listened to what my brother and my sister-in-law did not say in their living will. They did not name you as co-guardian to Joc..."

She glared at him, demanding he acknowledge the six-month-old as her own person, not just a name on a piece of paper.

"Jo-Jo. They made no provision for you to take care of the baby."

"But I *have* been taking care of her!" She looked at him imploringly. "Please, Carlo, Jo-Jo needs me."

He frowned, like her easy agreement angered him instead of pleasing him. "Meet me for dinner tomorrow night and we will discuss options."

"But I was going to go back to Upstate New York tonight, for Jo-Jo."

"She has Pamina. The baby will be fine."

Annette hoped that was true. Jo-Jo might be used to her father being gone during the week and seeing her own mother occasionally despite living in the same house, but for the last three months, Annette had been there all day, every day.

Nevertheless, she nodded. "Where do you want to meet?"

"I will send a car for you. Where are you staying?"

"I'm not. Like I said, I was planning to return on the train tonight."

"I will have a room booked for you at my hotel."

"Okay."

"No arguments about paying your own way or choosing your own lodgings?"

She stared at him. "None of that matters right now."

Annette wasn't even sure she *could* book her own hotel right now. She was beyond exhausted and doubted she'd sleep any better tonight than she had been since news had reached her of Joyce and Fantino's accident.

Chapter Nine

Carlo called his father after his nightly phone call with the nanny. Pamina had said Jo-Jo wasn't settling and had been fractious since lunchtime.

He'd asked if he needed to dispatch a doctor to check on the infant. The nanny had said no that she thought it was simply a matter of Jo-Jo missing Annette. "She's used to her aunt being there all of the time from what I've seen. She doesn't want to accept substitutes," Pamina had said.

Carlo had mentioned that opinion to his father and been shocked at the older man's response. "Of course, the baby misses her. Annette is practically the only mother she's known these past three months."

"What do you mean?" Carlo demanded. How much had Fantino neglected to tell him?

Was it because for the past five years, Carlo had made it clear he expected his family not to mention Annette to him?

He'd tolerated the occasional and inevitable times he would see her in person once Fantino and Joyce became serious about each other, but Carlo wanted no reminders of the most humiliating and *sì*, painful, episode in his life.

Not that he would ever admit to the emotional pain. He'd locked it away and chalked the relationship up as a learning experience.

But the cost of that learning experience had been steep. Not only had he nearly lost his father, but then a distant cousin had tried to take over the company because of Carlo's notoriety and the rumors circulating about him after he was jilted at the altar.

"Joyce was too ill to be a parent. You know this."

Only Carlo hadn't. Fantino had never said anything of the sort when they spoke or texted. The first he'd heard of the clinic had been today.

"She rejected Jo-Jo completely," his father went on, his voice heavy with sadness. "Fantino said she had postpartum depression. That's why he took her to California. He checked her into a clinic there that specializes in treatment of severe cases."

"And Joyce's case was that serious?" Fantino had never once mentioned his wife's illness to Carlo, and Carlo did not understand why.

"*Sì*. So severe she had thoughts of hurting both herself and her daughter. Without Annette's help, Fantino would have drowned under the pressure and Jo-Jo would not have thrived. Annette tried to help Joyce without professional intervention, but things were getting worse, not better. Fantino told me when they left for California that Joyce had not so much as held Jo-Jo in several days and she struggled to get out of bed each day."

Well, that explained why Fantino hadn't opened up about what was going on after the birth of his daughter. Carlo may have gotten a little over the top when Annette's name had been mentioned for the past five years.

None of his family knew about the sexual relationship that had started at the wedding. He hadn't wanted anyone assuming he was getting back together with her, but he could see now he should have at least told Fantino he and Annette were *friends* again.

Not that she had been acting very friendly the past couple of months. Ever since that less than successful video chat, she'd been ignoring his texts and phone calls.

"You know Annette took a leave of absence from work to take care of the baby and help her sister?" his father asked. "I think she had plans to move back to New York."

Stunned, Carlo did not answer. He had *not* known.

That was not the story Annette's father had been spinning to Carlo the past months. Moreover, his on-again-off-again lover had never mentioned plans to move across country, much less take time away from her job to care for their niece.

"I hadn't known that, actually. I thought she only came to watch Jocinda when they left for California."

"Oh, not at all. I know you have your reasons for thinking less of Annette, but she's been a good sister to Joyce and a loving aunt to my granddaughter."

"I wish Fantino had told me." His younger brother could have told him about Joyce's illness at the very least. They could have gotten in home therapy, or something.

"He didn't want you thinking less of him."

"Why would I?"

"Because he thought less of himself. He left Joyce on her own during the week, staying near the office in the city. He only went to her and the baby on the weekends and he thought her depression was his fault."

Apparently, his brother and father had discussed the difficulties going on extensively, but Fantino had not once brought them up to Carlo. According to Annette, Fantino had initially been the one to call and ask her to come help with the baby.

And he had not said word one to Carlo.

"He could have taken time off." Carlo hated knowing his younger brother had not been willing to share his difficulties with him. "I would have covered for him."

"He didn't want to take time off." His father's tone held resignation, not censure for her younger son's choices. "He spent the first two weeks in California with Joyce, but after that he flew back to visit her on the weekends."

The company had been both men's lives since they reached adulthood, and for the first time Carlo had to ask himself if that was best. He rang off with his father, his mind busy reframing the past three months with what he knew now. That video call and its outcome made a lot more sense.

Annette had been furious because he had misconstrued her motives and her actions. All based on her father's say so. A man whom Carlo had never considered unbiased when it came to his children. He and his wife played favorites, making it clear they did not feel the same way about their middle child as the other two.

Had she been an oops baby, or something? He'd always wondered, but never asked, not wanting to hurt Annette's feelings pointing out her parents' lack of affection.

Carlo had a great deal of work to do in his brother's office before he could sleep that night, but he found himself thinking about the only woman he had ever asked to marry him. His current lover, though he thought she was doing her best to avoid that role lately.

Because she'd been overwhelmed taking care of Jo-Jo, or because she was tired of him?

She'd turned off him easily enough five years ago. He wished his own craving for her was so easy to turn away.

He'd been shocked when she stood him up at the altar and he'd almost welcomed the media storm that followed because it had got his pride up and he hadn't gone chasing after her as had been his first inclination. By the time he'd dealt with the fallout of his botched attempt at marriage, he'd had no such inclination.

But just as he'd known might happen, the minute he'd seen her, he'd started wanting her again. This time, he'd been careful not to set up expectations. No strings sex.

And still, it had *hurt* when she stopped answering his texts and phone calls, when she cut him out of her life as he had once cut her out of his.

An idea began to form, a way for Carlo to finally get a little of his own back against the woman who had very nearly cost him his beloved father and the company that had been in their family for generations. A woman who had rejected him not once, but twice.

First as a husband, and then more recently as a lover.

Not because she didn't want him, he was sure of it. She responded too strongly to his touch for that to be the case, but because she'd discovered she wanted the strings of relationship she'd so cavalierly cut five years ago. She'd said as much in Sicily at the Christening.

A woman who had humiliated and betrayed him, making him an object of pity and anecdote to his Sicilian family and the media.

How the mighty are fallen. That's what several cousins had said, one in particular before trying the takeover bid. That man was selling cars in Rome now, and off every guest list Carlo was on, family, or no family.

Even being a billionaire is no protection from heartache, others had said, meaning well perhaps, but flaying Carlo's pride nonetheless.

Heartache? Five years ago, he had been far from some lovestruck teen, but he'd been painted as a tragic figure by his family and the media. Turned into an object of pity.

Carlo had hated it.

Now, here she sat, in a prime position for him to get what he wanted for himself, and for his baby niece. All of it on *his* terms.

A small niggle of worry said he was tired and stressed and should think before following through on his fantasies, but he ignored it.

The idea of getting anything on his terms seemed like a colossal joke the next day when he got Annette's text saying she was taking the train back to Upstate New York. He could come there and talk about her role in their niece's life while Jo-Jo's parents were still in hospital.

Feeling very much like he was chasing the wind, Carlo had his executive team shift things in his schedule and took the helicopter to Fantino's home, arriving shortly before Annette.

Annette searched out Jo-Jo, the minute she arrived back at the mansion, finding the baby playing with the rattles and things hanging above her plushy blanket on the floor in her nursery while Pamina read a book in the rocking chair.

With no thought to the business suit she'd worn to go into the City, Annette laid down on the carpet beside her niece and started talking to her. "What do you think of that giraffe? He looks like he would be fun to play with. Can you make him rattle?"

Jo-Jo's head turned at the sound of Annette's voice and then joyous baby babble filled the air between them. Dressed in cute, flowered stretchy pants and a long sleeved top with a big flower in the middle, Jo-Jo looked up at her aunt with joy in her sweet gaze. Her little feet covered in fuzzy booties kicked a mile a minute.

"Oh, she's happy to see you. I told *Signore* Messina our little Jo-Jo was missing you." Pamina's voice reminded Annette that someone else was in the room.

Annette looked up and smiled. "It's very good to be back." And she wasn't leaving.

If possession was nine tenths of the law, Annette was going to bolster it with squatter's rights. She wasn't going anywhere until Joyce came home to take care of her baby.

"I should have known you would come straight to the nursery." Carlo's voice came from the doorway.

She sat up, trying to keep her straight skirt from hiking up her legs. "You're here!"

"As you see."

"But I thought you were spending the day in New York."

"And I thought we had dinner plans. Apparently, we were both wrong."

Annette felt heat creep into her face, but she refused to be embarrassed. "I wanted to see Jo-Jo. I can't wait for Joyce and Fantino to be moved out of the ICU so we can take Jo-Jo to see them. I know hearing the baby talk will help."

"She doesn't talk yet, surely," Carlo said with disbelief.

"Well, not talk...but she babbles. It lifts my heart when I hear it. I know it will affect her parents the same, even in their comas."

Carlo's expression flashed pain and grief, but it was soon gone. Mr. Stoic. He nodded. "I am sure you are right."

"Perhaps you could finish your visit with our niece and then meet me in the study later?"

"She'll be ready for her nap soon," Pamina said.

Annette frowned but nodded. She didn't want to upset Jo-Jo's schedule. The baby had had enough discontinuity in her six months of life already.

An hour later, after changing into clothes that fit her style way better than the business suit, Annette went down to the study to meet with Carlo.

He was on the phone when she entered, so she turned to go out again, but he shook his head and waved her into a chair. He said something in Japanese and then tapped his phone screen.

"I'll be finished here in just a couple of minutes. Mrs. Banning has already laid lunch out on the table in the dining room. I thought we could have our discussion over a meal."

"Still looking for your dinner date?" she quipped.

"It's lunch and not a date." His tone was a lot more serious than hers. But then he went back to his call, and she took that as permission to leave.

Annette took a few minutes to chat with Mrs. Banning about the coming week before entering the formal dining room, where the table had been laid at one end.

Memories of stilted meals with her sister in here while Joyce did her best to pretend she didn't even have a baby bothered Annette. She knew her sister hadn't meant it, that hormones had dictated how she responded to life and her infant, but the memories still hurt. Especially with Joyce unable to come home and start bonding with Jo-Jo as planned.

"You look like you've seen a ghost. What is wrong?" Carlo asked upon entry into the room.

"It's not my favorite room, that's all."

"It's a dining room."

"Yes, I know." One with memories she'd rather forget.

"Would you prefer to eat our lunch somewhere else?"

It was too cold outside, and the breakfast nook was no doubt being used by the staff to eat their own lunch. Besides, the food was already laid out. "No of course not. I wouldn't put anyone to the bother."

"But something about this room bothers you."

"Joyce insisted on eating in here and when we were at the table, she didn't want Jo-Jo mentioned."

"But she was so happy to become a mom."

"Yes, but her hormones betrayed her." Annette shivered. "It's hard to accept how a chemical in your body can make a person think things that are so different than their true feelings, or do and say things they would otherwise never do."

Carlo looked at her speculatively. "Were you having hormone imbalances five years ago?"

"No. At least I don't think so." She settled into one of the chairs at the table and started dishing up her plate from the gorgeous Greek salad with smoked salmon Mrs. Banning had left for them.

Annette had been craving fish lately. She could eat it every day and be happy. Mrs. Banning had teased her about it, but the wonderful housekeeper had still prepared this mouthwatering salad with salmon instead of chicken as she usually did.

"Does it matter? Now?" Annette asked him, forcing herself to wait for him to sit down and serve himself before taking a bite of the salmon.

"No. It is water under the bridge as you Americans are so fond of saying."

Was that an American saying? Annette thought she'd look up its etymology later, but she doubted he would care the origination of the saying when he'd gotten it from his American business associates and friends.

"How was the train ride up?" he asked her.

As a subject change it was not inspired, but it was obvious. Once again, he had no interest in discussing their past in any meaningful way.

Annette tucked into her lunch. "These garlic bread knots taste as delicious as they smell."

Again, an uninspired topic for conversation, but a safe one.

Carlo waited until they'd eaten most of their lunch before broaching the topic he meant to.

Annette had shown a willingness to keep their conversation on totally inane topics, which revealed how nervous she was about their conversation to come, even if she didn't realize it. She'd expressed her near manic need to care for their niece the day before. Her emotions had been all but out of control, shocking him.

Funny how five years ago he would have told anyone who cared to listen that Annette was both sensible and practical, in everything but her choice of attire. She loved her whimsical clothing pieces, usually purchased at market stalls, not in high end department stores.

Now, he wondered if the way she always made sure everything was running smoothly, and never reacted with anger to her family's foibles, was more a result of family dynamic than personality and her way of dressing was Annette showing her true nature.

Dismissing the speculation, he observed, "You seem calmer today."

"Yesterday was a shock. I thought I was attending a meeting with the lawyer to go over things like finances for Jo-Jo's care and long-term plans for our siblings, and honestly, I resented having to take time away from the baby for something I thought you could handle. *That's* why I thought the rest of you were there. It never occurred to me that anyone *but me* would be named the baby's guardian."

"Nevertheless, I was named her legal guardian while her parents are unable to see to her care."

"I know." She frowned at him like she did not appreciate the reminder.

"I have a proposition for you."

Annette swallowed and nodded. "I understand."

"I doubt it, but you will."

Chapter Ten
Chapter 10

"What do you mean? You can't expect to take Jo-Jo back to Sicily," Annette asked with clear disapproval.

"None of us will be leaving New York until..." He let his voice trail off, unwilling to voice the options.

Until one, or both of, their siblings woke up and began to recover...or died.

"That's what I thought, but then you said you had a proposition..." her voice trailed off, her expression quizzical.

"I want you in my bed." There, he'd said it.

Though a voice inside him, which sounded suspiciously like his brother, called him a fool and demanded he retract the demand that she pay for the chance to care for their niece with her body. He didn't mean it. He knew he didn't mean it, but did she?

"What?" Shock held Annette's lovely face immobile.

"I think the strings of shared guardianship should satisfy your need for something more than casual sex."

"You want me to pay for the privilege of taking care of Jo-Jo with my body?" She laughed in disbelief, when he expected an air clearing explosion.

Why was she laughing instead of angry? Did she think he was joking?

"Those are my terms." But were they? Even as he said the words, his conscience squirmed.

Annette shook her head. "You have to know you don't have to blackmail me into your bed."

"You've ignored my every text and phone call for the last three months," he pointed out.

"Didn't like that much, huh?"

"No."

"I didn't like it when you did the same to me."

"Was it payback?"

"No. I was furious with you for ignoring the serious issues here and listening to my father about me."

"What is the deal with your parents?" He was sure she already realized that Carlo had had the wrong end of the stick during that conversation, so he didn't belabor the point.

"Maybe someday I'll tell you."

In other words, she didn't trust him enough to do it now. Could he blame her? He'd just tried to blackmail her into his bed. And she'd said it wasn't necessary.

"So, you intended to call me again?"

"I did, but I meant to offer you my own bargain."

"Oh?" Intrigued and growing increasingly uncomfortable with *his* bargain as stated, he was more than willing to entertain hers.

"Strings. I want strings."

"Shared guardianship," Carlo reminded her.

"What does that mean, exactly?"

"We will live here, together, with Jo-Jo, for the present."

"Only we share a bedroom."

Said like that, it sounded way less messy and even less ugly than the thoughts that had entertained him the night before. "Exactly. I am not promising a lifetime. In fact, it is my plan to get you out of my system. I want what my brother had, even if it ended badly. A wife who adores me, children. A family."

As he said the words, that same small voice he'd done such a good job ignoring so far asked why she couldn't be that woman? He'd changed in five years, maybe she had too. Maybe she regretted jilting him.

"And you have to get me out of your system for that to happen?" she asked, her tone odd and her expression unreadable.

"Apparently." But he was seriously beginning to doubt if he would *ever* get this woman entirely out of his system.

"Only you do expect our liaison to end sooner than later?"

"I do not know how long it will last," he replied truthfully. More honest than he'd been to this point.

But then if she knew him as well as he'd believed she had at one time, Annette was perfectly aware that he would never refuse her help with Jo-Jo. Their niece's welfare came first.

She sighed and put down her fork, finished with her lunch. "All right," she said, almost to herself, her focus on the table. Then she looked up and met his eyes. "Yes."

"Yes, what?" Was she agreeing to his ludicrous proposal?

"Yes, I'll be your lover for the foreseeable future."

"But..."

"Do we have to discuss terms right now?"

He shook his head, reeling from her easy acquiescence.

Something inside Carlo went cold at the knowledge she had just agreed to become his lover in exchange for a role in their niece's life. The old adage to be careful what he wished for filled his brain with biting clarity.

"What is the catch?" he asked, hoping there was one.

Because that at least would prove she understood his character even a little.

That damn shrug again. "Is there one?"

"No."

"You seem angry."

"Do I?" He shoved his plate away.

"Yes, but you are getting what you want." She smiled, almost teasing, if he could believe it. "Me."

"Or the use of your body," he pointed out.

Her smile did not dim. "And I am getting the use of yours."

"I have a contract I want you to sign."

"A contract?" *That* seemed to throw her.

"Knowing me as well as you do, I am surprised you did not expect one."

"I suppose that is true. It just feels odd having contract terms for something so personal."

"Come with me to the living room. I have the contract in there." There was an edge to Carlo's tone that Annette did not understand.

She asked, "Not the study?"

He just shook his head.

There was a neat stack of papers on the coffee table nearest the fireplace.

Oddly, Carlo took a moment to light the gas fire before joining her on the sofa in front of it. Like he was setting a cozy mood, only too much anger made his body rigid and his expression grim for any kind of warm atmosphere to prevail.

Annette took the proffered seat beside him and began to read the contract. As she read the over the multiple page document, her amusement just grew and grew. "I cannot believe you put this stuff down on paper."

It was obvious the contract had been written by him, not a legal team. There had been an attempt to make the document feel like a legal contract with binding this and first party that, but some of the clauses came straight out of Carlo's fantasies.

He'd gotten very specific about what he wanted in bed and out of it. There was something endearing about that. Even more so because from Carlo's expression, he expected her to be horrified.

And it occurred to Annette that everything to this point about the *deal* had been offered to get a reaction from her and she hadn't given the one he expected.

Unsure why that was the case, she simply pointed out, "You do realize none of this had to be put in writing, don't you? You have to know how much I want you, and we were never boring lovers before."

Annette wasn't ashamed of her desire and saw no reason to pretend otherwise.

"Will you sign it?"

She grinned up at him. "If you say so, but I'm pretty sure no judge in the country would hold me to these terms. I'm not even sure it's legal to put them down like this."

"You will honor your word."

"Will I? Only I thought you didn't trust me like that anymore." She couldn't help the taunt, not when it was becoming obvious to her that his intent here had been to get some of his own back in the humiliation department.

She didn't feel humiliated, but that was beside the point.

Carlo did not respond to her words.

Annette went back to reading, her amusement taking a sudden nosedive when she reached the terms outlining her responsibilities and rights with Jo-Jo. As she read the final clause, her heart stopped in her chest and then started pounding again. So fast, she thought she might faint from the blood rush.

In the event of the death of both of Jocinda's parents, the second party (Annette) agreed not to sue for custody of the child.

Everything inside Annette froze. "You put it in writing." She was so upset, her words came out in a hoarse whisper from the strain of pushing them past a tight throat. "That they could *die*."

She surged to her feet and glared down at him, tears already burning in her eyes. "You put it in writing! How could you do that?" Nowhere near whispering now, she swiped at the tears already running down her cheeks. "How could you say that? They aren't going to die!"

Joyce couldn't die. It wouldn't be fair. Life wasn't fair. But this was Joyce. The one person in Annette's life who truly loved her. A woman who was finally ready to be a mom and bond with her baby when fate had sent her to the hospital in a coma instead.

Suddenly, Annette could not breathe. The walls of the huge room were closing in on her, the fire so hot sweat prickled along her spine.

Spinning away, she ran from the room.

Carlo followed, calling her name.

Annette ran faster, rushing up the stairs, her eyes blinded by moisture. She tripped, falling backward, terror gripping her as she swung her arms wildly, trying to catch hold of something.

But it was Carlo who caught hold of her, stopping her fall. She wrested herself from his arms.

He put his hands out again. "Be careful, *bèdda mia*!"

She ignored him, turning and continuing her headlong rush toward her room.

"You were supposed to get mad about the other, yell at me. You never do what I expect..." Carlo's voice trailed after Annette, but she was no longer listening.

Her need to find the solitude and privacy of her room had morphed to an acute physical emergency. If she didn't get to the en suite, she would throw up all over her sister's plush carpet.

Annette made it to the toilet just in time, losing her lunch and then a dry heaving that resulted in nothing but pain and difficulty catching her breath. Carlo was there the whole time, offering her a glass of water, trying to calm her with words that didn't matter.

The only words that mattered were the ones he'd put in that darned contract.

A cold cloth settled on the back of her neck, a hand rubbed circles between her shoulder blades. The heaving finally stopped and Annette could drink the water, but first she rinsed her mouth and took in several deep lungfuls of air.

Carlo squatted beside her, finally silent.

She turned to glare balefully at him. "They aren't going to die."

"We have to be prepared for—"

"No," she cut him off without mercy. "We don't. We believe for them. We have to."

He nodded, looking like he was observing a particularly volatile creature, he wasn't sure how to deal with.

"I thought the stress nausea was gone. No thanks to you for bringing it back."

"Stress nausea?" he asked carefully.

"When I first got here. Things were rough. I was nauseated all the time, but it got better when Joyce got better."

"That was a little over three months after the Christening?" he asked, his tone curiously flat and his expression blank.

"Yes, I guess so. Does it matter?"

"Probably not." He shook his head, like he was clearing it. "I've been imagining all sorts lately."

"No, what are you trying to get at?" Had there been a bout of flu or something that went around after she left Sicily? Why would it have affected her so long?

"I'd say you were showing signs of pregnancy if you didn't have an IUD. Mrs. Banning said you were exhausted the first few weeks you were here, that you'd only started looking like you were getting your sleep recently. You still have dark circles under your eyes."

"Don't we all?" From what she'd seen of the two families at the lawyer's office, Annette didn't think anyone was getting enough sleep since news came of the accident.

"Yes, of course, you are right. I have not been myself lately, either."

Was that his oblique way of saying that the Carlo she knew would never have written that contract?

"I'm not signing your ridiculous sex contract."

"I never expected you to." He sighed, suddenly looking even more weary than before. "I wrote it when I was tired and maybe I'd had one too many glasses of whiskey from my brother's stash in his office. Writing that contract was a stupid thing to do."

"And you showed it to me why?"

His chiseled features reddened, but he just shook his head.

"You wanted to humiliate me," she guessed.

Sex hadn't given him closure. Maybe this had.

"You were not humiliated." He sounded disgruntled, but also kind of in awe of her.

Her lips tilted in a half smile. "No. You missed out on your bit of revenge for being stood at the altar. Poor you."

"That is not the way I see it."

"If you don't rip it up, I'm going to ask Mrs. Banning to burn your breakfast every day until you go back to Sicily."

Annette wasn't leaving those words about Joyce and Fantino's possible deaths in writing. She did not care if it was rational. Annette did not feel rational. She felt terrified. Terrified of losing Joyce permanently. Frightened for Jo-Jo and what the baby's future held.

"Your plans for revenge are so much more prosaic than mine." Carlo sounded admiring.

On that, they could agree. "But effective. You don't do well without a proper breakfast."

"You know me well, or I thought you did."

"And now you've decided that I don't?" Annette heaved herself up from the floor and washed her face with cold water before drinking some more water.

Her stomach felt settled, but for how long? The source of her stress was standing right in front of her.

"You were going to sign the contract."

"Until I read that clause. How could you put that in there?"

"I was being thorough."

"And the list of sexual fantasies wasn't thorough enough?"

He grimaced, high cheekbones burnishing an even deeper red. "That was..." He waved his hand. "It was late at night when I wrote that. I had been working nonstop for days and I had not slept properly since leaving Sicily. I thought you would be offended by the sex stuff, yell at me..."

He'd said something like that when she'd been running for her room.

Annette sidestepped Carlo and went into the bedroom, but then she stopped, just looking around, unsure what she wanted to do now. Jo-Jo would not be up from her nap for another hour. She still slept longer in the afternoon than during morning nap time.

"Why would you want me to yell at you?" she asked him.

Because of course Carlo had followed her, like he'd been doing since she dashed out of the dining room.

"I wanted some of my own back. I will not deny it," he said stoically, like admitting a huge secret but doing it *manfully*. "But I also thought you would yell and I would yell and we would clear the air on five years ago."

"That's..." She didn't know what that was. Ludicrous? Only not. "But I've offered to talk about what happened back then several times and you've insisted we already drew a line under it."

He shrugged. "I am Sicilian. I am proud."

"And you needed to be angry to talk about something that hurt you deeply."

"I never said I was hurt."

No, but he'd never been willing to talk about it at all.

"I don't want to have to have an argument to talk. My body's taken to handling stress through my stomach."

Again with the look. "An IUD is more than 99% effective, but there are outliers."

"True. I don't have an IUD anymore though."

"You don't?" he asked, his tone laced with shock. "But I thought..." He shook his head, like thinking better of what he'd been about to say.

"When the last one expired, I didn't have another put in. I wasn't in a relationship, or sexually active. How is this any of your business?" she demanded, realizing she was rambling personal details she wasn't sure she wanted to share with Mr. Get-Her-Out-Of-His-System.

"It is not, except that we had in person, penetrative sex when you were in Sicily. Quite a bit of it and I was unaware we were relying entirely on condoms for birth control."

"You didn't ask."

"No, I didn't. I'm not assigning blame, merely explaining."

"What exactly?"

"Why I think you should take a pregnancy test."

Chapter Eleven
Chapter 11

Carlo would have smiled at the stupefied expression on Annette's face, but in her current state of emotional volatility, he wasn't taking any chances in her misinterpreting his smile.

"But we always used a condom."

"All birth control has a failure rate, even when used perfectly, and I admit I wasn't as careful, believing you had an IUD." He realized he was mansplaining to a woman who worked with at risk youth.

Annette's knowledge of birth control no doubt outstripped his by miles. However, she was acting like the idea of pregnancy had never occurred to her.

"I can't be pregnant," she said, shaking her head as if her will alone could repudiate the possibility. "Joyce and Fantino are in comas. Jo-Jo needs me right now. I...It's..."

"Your choice, naturally."

She stared at him. "Yes, I...wait, I don't want. Nothing I'm saying is making sense, is it?"

"You are upset."

"Yes, but I'm also a grown up. You're right. I need a pregnancy test. Then we can talk about what's what."

He knew what *he* wanted, but Carlo didn't fool himself into believing it was the same as what she did. She'd jilted him five years before, and unless something had drastically changed for her, happy families was not in their future.

"And just to clarify something. I do know you. I never doubted you would let me stay with Jo-Jo because that's what's best for her and you would never do anything less. I agreed to become your lover because I wanted to. Full. Stop."

Flummoxed, Carlo watched Annette walk out of the room, not a single word in answer coming to his lips.

She'd been prepared to sign that ridiculous contract because she wanted to be his lover and for no other reason.

Carlo went to the pharmacy and bought the pregnancy test, leaving it in Annette's room before going in search of her. He found her returning with a bundled-up Jo-Jo from their walk.

Pamina stepped forward and offered to remove Jo-Jo's outer clothes for Annette.

Her cheeks rosy from the cold and her hair windswept, Annette nodded. "If you don't mind, bring her down to the kitchen and I'll feed her before her bath."

Despite everything, Carlo's body reacted like it always did to Annette's presence. Desire coursed through him as she undid her own outer layers in a thoroughly unsexy striptease that nevertheless resulted in him having to adjust his stance, so his arousal wasn't too noticeable.

Annette noticed anyway. Her eyes widened. "What's that about?" She nodded toward his erection. "Developed a fetish for the outdoorsy vibe?"

"I want you in all your vibes. I thought we'd established that."

"Are you saying you haven't been with anyone else?"

He was not sure how she drew that conclusion from his words, but it was true. "Not in a long time, no."

"What? You've got gorgeous women on your arm at every social function."

"Not every date ends in bed."

"Ours always did."

"That should tell you something."

"That we're sexually compatible." She waved with her hand. "That's chemistry. It doesn't mean much."

"It meant a lot to me five years ago."

"But not now. You're the one who said he wanted to get over me so you could go looking for the perfect paragon to marry."

"I never used that term and naturally, if you are pregnant, my plans will change."

"You think so?" she asked enigmatically.

"I do think so." Carlo spoke with all the arrogant confidence at his disposal.

It had always been his policy to begin as he meant to go on. And if she was pregnant, he meant to marry her.

Annette was getting ready for bed when a firm knock sounded on her door. She hurried into her sleep pants and grabbed a cardigan to put on over her sleep tank before opening the door.

Carlo stood on the other side, his gorgeous face cast in expectation. "Well?"

"What?" Then she realized and grabbed his arm, tugging him into her room.

She wasn't having this conversation out in the hall.

Annette shut the door and locked it for good measure. "I'm not taking the test until tomorrow morning. They're most accurate when used first thing in the morning."

She didn't mention that was mostly true for testing early in a pregnancy and if she'd gotten pregnant in Sicily, Annette would now be almost four months along. She'd had a short period that first month and none since, but her periods had been sporadic since taking out the IUD. Her body was still adjusting, or so her doctor assured her.

Annette certainly didn't mind the months she got to skip her monthly.

"Oh. I had not realized."

"Why would you? Unless you'd thought you'd gotten other women pregnant." She looked at him expectantly.

"No. Never." Carlo looked at her attire and smiled. "Interesting pajamas."

Her cardigan was dark orange, her sleep pants were lime green and her sleep tank was grey with a black and white picture of iconic cartoon characters kissing on the front. Under were the words, *closet romantic*.

"I wasn't expecting company."

"Weren't you?"

"No. I thought you might wait until we knew for sure on the pregnancy thing before launching the seduction offensive."

"There is nothing offensive about my seduction techniques," he assured her.

No, there really wasn't.

"You haven't been with anyone else while we were having our *friends with benefits* thing?" she asked, wondering what it meant if he said no.

"Not since before the wedding," he offered.

"What about the no strings, it was just a one-night stand, yadda yadda yadda?"

"I have never said yadda in my life and I have no answer for you. I did not believe myself committed to you and yet I had no desire to have sex with other women."

Why did he say bone melting things right along with the cold hard truth? "You said you wanted to get closure. To be able to move on. Are you saying that having sex with other women hasn't worked for you since our breakup?"

Because that would put them in the same boat, and she wasn't sure how she felt about that. She'd been the one to walk away (or more accurately run away) five years before. If she hadn't, what would their life be like now?

"Have there been other men?" he asked, rather than give a straight answer.

Typical Carlo.

"None successfully."

Something flared in his eyes. Was it satisfaction or relief? Or both?

"Why should it matter?" she asked. But she knew.

For the same reason she liked knowing his sex life hadn't been great since they broke up.

A very primal part of Annette still saw Carlo as hers. She wanted to be the only woman who spurred him to all night long intimacy.

"You know," he said, moving into her personal space. "You feel it too."

Annette's breath caught, her body suffusing with heat that had nothing to do with embarrassment. She wanted him.

She always wanted him. And he always wanted her.

Wasn't that something worth pursuing? She'd downplayed the power and importance of the chemistry between them earlier, but after five years of unsuccessful and mostly nonexistent (because of the unsuccessful part) dating, she now knew just how rare that kind of sexual compatibility was.

Annette tipped her head back, so their gazes met. His simmered with desire.

She knew he could see a matching need in her own.

"I do feel it."

He smiled, white teeth flashing in that sexy way that got her every time. "This." He cupped her waist beneath her cardigan, his big hand warm through the thin cotton of her sleep tank. "But you feel the other too. You like being the woman I can't get out of my head."

"More like your pants, but yes."

"I'm going to kiss you."

"I'm going to let you."

She didn't see the smile that time because she'd closed her eyes as his lips met hers. She felt it though at the beginning of the kiss.

Kissing back with all the passion she had unwittingly banked for the past three and a half months, Annette shrugged out of her cardy before grabbing his hair and holding him in place for the kiss to go on and on and on.

He growled against her lips as he cupped her bottom with both hands, pulling her up his body so his sex aligned with the apex of her thighs. Annette wrapped her legs around him, rubbing herself against his hardness.

Oh, how she'd missed this. And no way was it all about sex.

Not when neither of them could manage satisfying sex with anyone else.

But that was a thought for another time. Annette's body felt on fire with need to be touched, every nerve ending sparking the conflagration of need inside her.

She felt their bodies moving and then her back hit the familiar support of her bed. Only everything else about this was unfamiliar. Having a masculine body above her, rutting between her thighs even though they were both still fully clothed.

It took bare moments for that to change as they both threw their clothes off with abandon, needing to get to skin on skin.

He knelt above her, his hard honed body leashed with power, sexual need emanating off him in electric waves that connected to her body, creating a sexual current between them that only seemed to get more intense second by second. His sex jutted from his body, already glistening at the tip.

"You are so beautiful," he said, his gaze traveling all over her like the sexiest caress.

But she shook her head. "No, that's you."

His laugh was strained. "Always arguing with me."

"You wouldn't want things too easy." Though she was about to make things very easy for him. Or maybe very good. Easy wasn't all it was cracked up to be.

"No, if I wanted easy, I never would have fixed my sights on you, Annette."

She begged to differ. Five years ago. She'd been very accommodating. Until she wasn't.

Maybe not so easy after all.

"Right now, I want you to fix something."

"What is that?" he asked, cupping her breasts, kneading them and playing with her nipples in the way he knew drive her wild with need.

She told him, in intimate detail. One thing their video sex chats had done for Annette was obliterate her shyness about speaking her sexual needs aloud. It had made cybersex more intense and she realized from his ferocious reaction, it was going to do the same for in person intimacy.

When he stopped to don a condom saying, "If you are not pregnant, now is not the time to make decisions like this," she was filled with another feeling all together. Love.

He was taking care of her, and she had to admit that he always had. If sometimes in a very high-handed way they *would* have to talk about if she were pregnant and he thought that meant fulfilling the plans that she'd leveled five years ago.

He entered her and she surged upward to meet him, needing this connection to the very core of her being.

They made love, their passion building along with a certainty inside of Annette.

She was always going to want this man. If she was pregnant, they were going to have to find a way to make it work between them because she *was* too easy for this man.

Annette's climax hit her without warning and she screamed her pleasure even as Carlo found his own release, his shout ringing in her ears.

Later, cuddled into his body, the covers over them rather than under them, Annette said, "Well, even if no one saw you come into my room, everyone who lives here knows you've been in my bed now."

"Pamina and Mrs. Banning are the only staff that lives in." Carlo said it like it made all the difference that only two people and not twenty knew they'd just had sex.

"Mrs. Banning is the only one that matters. She'll tell Joyce for sure."

"I do not think so. She's an imminently respectable housekeeper. She wouldn't gossip about the household."

"First, respectability has nothing to do with it. Second, what era do you think we live in?" Though she wasn't convinced that staff had gossiped any less in past eras than they did now. "She and Joyce are friends. She'll tell her for sure."

He shifted so he was on his side looking at her in the shadowed moonlight. "Does that bother you?"

"Did you tell Fantino about us?" she asked him, playing his own trick back at him.

Question for question. No answers in evidence.

"I did not, and I regret that. Maybe he would have confided in me if I had."

"Why do you think neither of them named me as guardian, or even co-guardian, of Jo-Jo in the event they were both incapacitated?" She didn't say dead, because she was *not* saying that out loud.

Not with both of them still on some form of life support.

Carlo waited to answer, so she knew he was doing her the courtesy of really thinking about it. "I do not know. They made us both godparents. Why not name us both guardians?"

"Because they assumed I wouldn't drop everything to be here for them." She didn't wonder why they hadn't changed the wills they'd had drawn up when they'd gotten married.

There'd been no reason to believe two young, healthy people needed to update their will, even after she'd come to stay and care for Jo-Jo. They'd all believed everything would work out for Joyce.

It had. And then it hadn't.

It hurt more than she could express that Joyce, the one person she'd believed was her *true* family, the only one in her family who loved Annette, had not seen her as a good bet as her daughter's guardian.

"Perhaps your father influenced her. He seems to see through a cracked lens when looking at you."

"Not cracked, just not the same color as the one he has for his biological children."

Carlo went still, his expression unreadable in the dark. "What do you mean?"

Chapter Twelve

Unwilling to have this conversation without being able to see his reaction to her words, Annette reached out and turned on the lamp by the bed.

Then she sat up, pulling the bedding up to cover her naked breasts. Not because she was embarrassed by her nudity with him. How could she be? However, she didn't want this discussion derailed by sex. It was something she should have talked about with him five years ago.

"I'm adopted."

Carlo stared at her, his jaw going slack for the first time in their acquaintance. "Say again."

"I'm adopted," she repeated.

Sitting up, he made a visible effort to regain his usual composure. "And you have found this out recently?"

"I've always known." Then she explained about her father giving her to his brother when he wanted to remarry after her mother's death. "He paid my Father and Mother a monthly stipend for my care until I turned 18."

"That explains you having to work your way through university." There was something strange in Carlo's tone.

He was right though. She'd always known her parents wouldn't pay for it and Annette had worked hard to get a scholarship to make college even possible for her. She'd done it too. "They let me live in their home until I graduated."

"Generous of them." Sarcasm dripped from every word.

Annette shrugged. "I thought it was at the time. I knew I wasn't wanted, not by my biological father, not by them. Anything they were willing to give me felt like a gift."

"So, you tried to make a place for yourself by being useful."

The Cinderella complex the media had made such a meal of. He was right. "Not exactly. My mom didn't like the way I dressed, or how gauche I was with important people, so she'd send me back into the kitchen to make myself useful. None of us really had chores growing up, other than cleaning our rooms really. Only somehow, I always ended up doing stuff that Lynette didn't want to and Joyce was too young to do well. A last-minute cleanup of the guest bathroom before important visitors, and the like."

"But your parents had staff to do that sort of thing."

"Yes. But she kept the staff busy and my mom resented me. It didn't matter to her that the money she and Dad got for taking care of me was more than a nominal stipend, or that it made it possible for Dad to build his business."

"You never told me any of this."

"No."

"Why?"

"My parents did not allow us to talk about it. Lynette knew of course. She was six and I was five when my biological dad dumped me with his brother."

"What about Joyce?"

"She figured it out when she was a teenager, not long before we met."

"She never treated you any different."

"No, she didn't." Which was why her sister making Carlo her child's guardian with no mention of Annette hurt so much. "She always acted like I was her sister and that was that."

"She didn't make Lynette Jo-Jo's guardian either," Carlo pointed out, like he knew what she was thinking.

"Can you imagine? Lynette doesn't have a nurturing bone in her body. She's never made any bones about the fact she does not crave motherhood."

"That is not what she implied to me."

"She wanted to hook you."

"It did not work."

"No." And Annette felt a great deal of satisfaction at that truth.

"You kept an important truth about yourself from me. No wonder everything fell apart five years ago."

"I didn't back out of the wedding because I am adopted."

"Didn't you? Are you saying the insecurity you felt with your family did not contribute to you walking away from me?"

Annette opened her mouth, but no words came out. She couldn't deny that because she now knew that feeling unworthy of her family's love *had* been part of why she'd run away so far and so fast. She'd been certain he needed perfection and she'd never lived up to that with her family. How could she with him?

But had he needed her to be his perfect wife? Or had she played a part five years ago that somewhere deep inside she knew she couldn't keep playing for a lifetime?

Cinderella.

A woman who had been her family's perpetual servant and was destined to be an extension of her future husband rather than his partner.

"It was a secret," she reminded him now, rather than acknowledge the truth of his words out loud. "I wasn't supposed to tell anyone. Ever."

"You were going to marry me," he pointed out, like that mattered.

"I was ashamed." She hadn't realized that until therapy, but it helped Annette understand why she found it so easy to think everything was her fault.

"Of being adopted?"

She didn't answer for several seconds, looking for the words that hadn't come easily even in the therapist's office. "Of being unwanted. Unworthy of my father's love, of not being enough to inspire love in my adoptive parents."

"But your father's lack and frankly the lack of your parents now is not your fault."

"After three years of therapy, I mostly know that, but the feeling of shame is a hard one to shake. I work on it every day, reminding myself that my birth father didn't give me up because there was something wrong with me, but because he lacked something inside himself that allowed him to give up his five-year-old daughter without a backward glance."

"He was an ass."

She laughed, but privately agreed. Looking back at how her adoptive parents had treated her, she wasn't too impressed with their nurturing instincts either. Whatever their reasons for always finding the fault, the actual fault hadn't been in who she was, but who they wanted her to be.

The next morning, Annette peed on the stick and then stared at it in shock for several minutes before a knock sounded on the bathroom door.

For once, she'd been up well before Carlo, needing to do the test and show him she *wasn't* pregnant. Only, she was. Nearly four months along. Why wasn't she bigger? Her tummy looked the same, or maybe a little poochy, but Annette had always been curvy. Though goodness knew she'd tried for willow thin when she was younger, trying to look more like her tall, svelte adopted sisters and mom.

The knock sounded again. "Annette." Just that one word. Her name. No demand to be let inside though she knew he had to be itching to ask her if she'd taken the test yet.

"I took the test," she said through the door, strangely reluctant to open it.

"Let's talk about it."

Like they hadn't talked five years before. She got that. Annette wasn't a young and uncertain 22-year-old any longer. She knew how she fit in the world and accepted the things that could not be changed.

At least she thought she did.

She was pregnant.

That could be changed, but Annette really had no desire to take steps in that direction. She wanted this baby. Her baby. Carlo's baby. Family.

She opened the door, the stick still in her hand.

"What do the double blue lines mean?" he asked.

"Well on some tests, they would mean I'm not pregnant." She always taught her youth to read the instructions on the package because those lines and their colors meant different things to some of them.

"And on this one?" he pressed, standing there naked and every bit as confident as if he'd donned one of his bespoke suits.

"It means I'm going to have a baby."

"*Sì?*" he asked, excitement glinting in his grey gaze. "Am I allowed to celebrate?"

Was he? Was she? Annette's hand went to her stomach, and she smiled. "Yes, I think we are."

"You are going to have my baby." His eyes filled with moisture that shocked her. "I am undone."

And then he undid her with lovemaking that was so tender, it was her eyes that burned with emotion as she climaxed.

They were eating a late breakfast when Carlo's phone rang. He looked at the screen and went pale.

"What? What is it?" Annette asked.

He shook his head. "I do not know, but it is the hospital."

"Well, answer it! Maybe one of them has woken up." They had plans to visit the hospital later while Pamina watched Jo-Jo.

Somehow, Carlo had finagled an appointment with an obstetrician for her in the hospital complex as well.

"*Sì*. I mean, yes, it is Carlo Messina." His voice reverberated with stress.

He was not expecting good news, but Annette would not let herself consider anything else.

"He has? Yes. Yes. *Sì*. We will be there directly." He hung the phone up and looked at Annette, his expression filled with shock.

"What is it? Is Fantino...he's all right, isn't he? Did they have to take him back into surgery?"

"He woke up. He is awake." Carlo surged to his feet and came around to pull her up and into his arms. "He is awake. He is stable. They are moving him to a private room." He hugged Annette so hard she squeaked.

Releasing her immediately, he stared at her in abject horror. "*Scusami*! I am sorry. Did I hurt the baby?"

"No, you didn't hurt the baby. Or me." She wrapped her arms around him and hugged him back, hard. "I'm so happy. He's going to be okay."

"You always said, but I feared..." His voice choked off and she let him have his moment. Finally, he went on, his voice still clogged with emotion. "I feared the worse, but you did not. You had faith enough for us all."

She held onto Carlo tight, wishing her sister was awake as well but rejoicing no less in her heart for Fantino's start to recovery. "Can we take Jo-Jo to see him?"

"I do not know." Carlo stepped back, his usual urbane manner completely eclipsed by his relief at the news about Fantino. "I should have asked. Why did I not ask?" He rambled on in Sicilian.

"Do you want me to call your parents?" she asked.

If the hospital had called him, Carlo was the contact on file.

"*Sì. Sì*. We must call them."

"Okay, here's what's going to happen. You contact your executive team and deal with how this is going to impact your schedule. I'll call your mother. She'll tell your father."

"I have already cancelled my calls for today. We have our own appointment to attend."

"You are coming to the OB with me?" She'd just assumed she'd be going alone while he did business in the back of the limo like he'd done on some occasions when they were dating.

"Of course, I am going with you, unless you do not want me there? It is your choice, after all."

He kept saying that. It was her choice. And it was true. She appreciated that he recognized that. "Then if it is my choice, I would like you there."

She'd spent four months pregnant and not even realized. She wasn't feeling great about that and why his presence made her feel better she didn't choose to dwell on.

"*Bene*. You call my mother. She will cry all over you. I will call my father."

"As if he is not going to cry all over you," Annette teased.

Neither of them said anything about Carlo's own tears of relief and joy.

Annette's phone call with Valentina had gone much as Carlo thought it would. Valentina had interspersed her joy at her son's waking with tears and promises to Annette that Joyce would wake eventually too.

"These Sicilian tycoons, they are too cynical to believe like us, but we will hold faith for your sister."

Annette was so touched, she could barely get out a heartfelt, "Thank you."

"*Famigghia esti famigghia*," she said prosaically. "We are family, *sì?*"

Yes, they were family. And soon that tie would be made even stronger by a child. Carlo and Annette's child.

She and Carlo hung up with their calls about the same time.

"Your mother is overcome with joy," she said to him.

"My father also." He looked entirely too smug, so she should have guessed what was coming next. "He is also delighted to have another grandchild on the way."

"You told them?" she asked, her voice risen in shock. "Surely now is not the time for that news."

"It is the best time. It gives my father a reminder that life wins." He reached out and laid his hand over her belly. "Our baby is *my* reminder that life wins. Sometimes, life wins."

Not always. Not even Annette believed that, but yes sometimes life did win.

It certainly felt like it when they entered Fantino's hospital room later to find him already talking to his parents, who were staying at a hotel only minutes from the medical complex.

His smile when he saw his brother was beautiful to see, but then that same smile was turned to her. "Annette, our savior."

"How can you say that?" She shook her head, tears clogging her throat and washing into her eyes. She spun on her heel and rushed from the room.

She collapsed against the wall outside, unable to control the tears.

A hand landed on her shoulder, but it was not Carlo's as she'd expected. It was Valentina's. "There, child, let it out. You were not to blame for this accident. Whatever your parents said in their grief, they do not believe it either."

"They do." It wasn't just grief. It was lack of love.

"Then they are fools." Valentina's bald statement without trying to convince Annette otherwise came as a surprise that almost stopped her tears.

"Yes, you pushed for your sister to get help. And I am grateful for it. We are all grateful. She deserves to be happy in her motherhood, but that is not such an easy thing always."

"No," Annette choked out.

"Fantino knows Joyce is still in a coma. He needs us to remind him she will come out of it."

"Cynical tycoon." Annette was still crying, but not as hard. A golden tanned hand reached out with a box of tissues. Carlo.

Of course, the man who did not love her nevertheless always knew what she needed. Except when he didn't, she reminded herself.

Jilting him hadn't happened in a vacuum.

Annette took the tissue and mopped herself up. "Thank you."

"Are you alright?" Carlo's gaze searched her face. "Fantino wants to see you."

Annette nodded. "Yes, I just..."

"Carry too much inside. I will remember that even when you don't look like you are going off the rails like the rest of us, you are inside. I should have realized after that appointment with the lawyers, but then you were your usual feisty self. Now, I know."

What he thought he knew she wasn't entirely sure, but one thing stuck. Carlo had acknowledged going off the rails. That was big. He put his hand out and she took it, concentrating on the warmth of his clasp and not the hospital sounds and smells around them.

They re-entered the hospital room that looked more like a high-end hotel room, but for all the machines and the IV hanging to the right of the bed. Alceu made a place for her beside the bed and Annette forced herself to approach and then stand there, looking down at the man whom she loved like a brother.

And whom her advice had nearly killed.

Chapter Thirteen

"Annette, sister." Fantino's voice was not his usual strong tenor, but it was unmistakably his. "You saved my family."

"I..."

Fantino grasped her free hand. "Did not cross three lanes of traffic because you were too tired to be driving."

Annette stared first at Fantino and then at Alceu Messina, who looked back stoically. "You told him all of it, is that wise?"

"I remembered most of it," Fantino said.

"You wouldn't have been in California if not for me," she said. "I'm sorry. Carlo mentioned in home therapy, and it never even occurred to me."

"The decision to go to California was Joyce's and I agreed with it, even though it meant leaving our baby in your provenly capable hands. I want to see Jo-Jo." Fantino looked to his brother like he expected Carlo to make that happen.

"As soon as the doctor approves the visit, we will bring her." Carlo's voice rang like a promise in the room.

Fantino nodded, clearly satisfied. "Joyce will wake soon and she'll be annoyed I got to see Jo-Jo first."

"She's really looking forward to finally bonding with her baby," Annette said, doing her best to keep emotion from her voice and pretty sure she'd failed miserably.

"She is," Fantino agreed. "The treatment made such a difference for her. I got my wife back, thanks to you."

"You won't lose her," Annette said in as much a plea as a promise.

She could not stand losing her sister.

"No, I won't. She's more stubborn than me. She'll wake up soon."

Annette nodded, too overcome with emotion to get any words past her tight throat. Carlo seemed to know and pulled her into his body, his arm coming protectively around her.

Fantino looked at them with speculation. "Is there something you want to share with the class?"

"We are having a baby," Carlo said, his own tone suffused with joy at impending fatherhood.

He might not think she was great shakes as potential wife material, but he was ecstatic she was having his baby. And Annette knew now that it had been confirmed, whatever his previous plans, Carlo was now set on wooing her into a wedding.

Again.

Only this time, she wasn't living in the fantasy that he loved her. The fantasy that had popped like a soap bubble when he'd laid out his plans for their future without her input, or even taking her feelings into consideration.

"When's the wedding?" Fantino asked. "Only I don't recommend waiting like we did. The wedding was a lot of stress on Joyce in her last trimester."

"Now is not the time for a big wedding, regardless," Carlo said, his tone brooking no argument.

He wasn't going to get one from her. "I agree."

"But there will be a wedding?" Alceu asked, *his* tone equally intransigent.

Before Annette could stutter some kind of answer that basically said she wasn't sure, or Carlo could say whatever he'd just taken a breath to get out, his mother said, "Leave them alone, *caro*. Today is for celebrating Fantino's recovery. Tomorrow is time enough to begin badgering your eldest about his love life."

Fantino started to droop soon after that, so Annette and Carlo took their leave. Valentina refused to be moved and declared she would read while he slept.

Considering that the furniture in the hospital room was as comfortable as any Annette had had in her living room, she wasn't worried the older woman would make herself exhausted with a bedside vigil. Valentina deserved having whatever moments of wakefulness her son gave her throughout the day after the worry he would not wake at all.

Annette and Carlo looked in on Joyce and found Lynette there, reading to their younger sister from a fashion magazine. "You'll adore this new line from…" She let her voice trail off when she saw them. "What are you doing here?" she asked pointedly of Annette.

"She's my sister too," Annette said, wishing her older sister's words no longer had the power to hurt her.

She'd come a long way to believing it wasn't her fault her family didn't love her, but that didn't mean she didn't love them, or that they couldn't hurt her.

"I guess," Lynette said grudgingly, surprising Annette.

But then she chanced a side glance at Carlo and the glower he was giving her sister was pretty ferocious. Lynette was doing her best to avoid his gaze at this point.

Annette probably shouldn't feel like smiling, but she did. Lynette was so used to everyone being okay with the way she treated Annette; she didn't know what to do with herself when someone disapproved.

Lynette stood up abruptly. "If you're going to be here for a while, I'll take a walk."

"Have you been here all day?" Annette asked, surprised.

"Yes, not that you'd know. You barely bother to visit, despite living less than an hour away."

"I visit as much as I can, but Jo-Jo needs me right now."

"So you've said." Lynette flipped her highlighted brown hair. "She has a nanny. We all heard Carlo say so."

"And yet a nanny cannot substitute for family. The better question might be why neither your parents, nor yourself have taken the time to check on Jo-Jo's welfare during all this."

"She's fine. You said so yourself."

"But none of you stepped in to offer help in her care."

Lynette frowned. "Why would we? Joyce needs us. The baby has carers."

Her sister's blatant dismissal of their niece's needs didn't surprise Annette, but it did hurt. "Jo-Jo deserves to be surrounded by people who love her while her parents can't be there."

"If they ever wake up," Lynette said, genuine regret in her voice as she looked down at Joyce. "It has been more than two weeks."

"Fantino woke up earlier. It's just a matter of time before Joyce does," Annette said, believing it.

She had to believe it.

"What? Fantino's awake?" Lynette asked in shock and then she looked at Annette accusingly. "Why weren't we told?"

"By we you mean?" Carlo asked in a tone that wasn't exactly friendly.

Lynette didn't seem to notice. "Me and my parents. Joyce's family. Fantino is my brother-in-law."

"Annette is also Joyce's family, but as long as you refuse to acknowledge that you cannot expect to be in either my parents or my favor." It was a warning, clear as day.

Annette heard it. Lynette did too because the look she shot Annette was positively venomous.

"There are things you don't know," she said to Carlo. "Besides, she is the woman who jilted you at the altar five years ago and humiliated you in the process. Or had you forgotten?"

"I have forgotten nothing, least of which the role you played in the social and tabloid media storm that followed.

Lynette sucked in a breath, her mouth opening and closing like a fish. She was so obviously trying to think of what to say to spin the past in a different light, Annette almost felt sorry for her. Almost.

But while Lynette was undoubtedly a good sister to Joyce, she was not a nice person.

"As to apprising you of my brother's improved condition, my father called yours earlier today."

"Oh!" Lynette grabbed her phone out of her bag and said a word they would have been punished for uttering as teens. "I had my phone on silent. Dad texted me."

Annette knew she had gotten no similar text, but chose to believe that was because Alceu had told her father that she already knew.

Lynette turned to go, but before she could leave the room, Carlo said, "I know Annette is adopted and I know why. That does not reflect badly on her, but your family's behavior reflects very poorly on all of you."

The brunette spun and stared. "You told him?" she demanded of Annette, accusation in every syllable. "That's a family matter."

"That I am adopted is a *personal* matter and who I choose to tell is none of your business." Annette was done pretending her past was something to be ashamed of or hidden.

"But nobody wanted you. Why would you want people to know that?" Lynette asked, incomprehensibly.

"Our parents wanted me, or at least the money I could bring them. It was their choice not to love me, but that is not my fault." And finally, Annette believed that, to the very core of her.

Whatever was lacking in her family's feelings toward her, it came from a dearth in their own hearts, not in her.

"I didn't want a sister," Lynette said baldly. "Joyce was different, she was a cute baby and full of smiles for me, but you? That first year, you were either crying, or quiet and sullen. You ignored me."

"And you couldn't stand that." Annette shook her head. "It never occurred to you that I'd lost both my parents within a year of each other and the grief was overwhelming."

"I was six. Of course, I didn't think about that."

"But you are no longer six," Carlo pointed out.

"No." Lynette shook her head. "I got in the habit of resenting you and it never went away."

"We don't ever have to be friends, but maybe you could work on not being such a complete mess of a human?" Annette suggested.

"I'm not a mess. I just don't like you."

About to quip that the feeling was entirely mutual, Annette cast a quick glance toward the bed, guilt immediately wracking her for having this discussion at her sister's bedside. What she saw nearly sent her to her knees.

Joyce's eyes were open. And they were clear. Her hand not tethered to an I.V. was moving toward her face like she wanted to grab the apparatus there.

Annette leaped toward the bed, but her hand was gentle when she put on her sister's wrist. "Don't. They'll take it out for you. You are okay. It is all going to be okay."

Joyce looked at her with trust and a lot more alertly than Annette expected.

The doctors had said that Fantino took a couple of hours to become fully coherent, but Joyce's eyes were clear.

Lynette rushed to the bed. "You're awake."

Joyce shifted her head slightly toward Lynette's voice and winced.

"Shh...shh...don't move just yet. Let the doctor and nurses check you over," Annette said.

"I've got to tell Mom and Dad." Lynette left the room to make the call.

Joyce's eyes followed her.

"She's been with you almost every day," Annette said. "Give her a minute to get herself together. You know she doesn't like for anyone to see her cry."

Joyce blinked, but her eyes asked questions.

"There was an accident. Do you remember?"

Joyce's expression filled with horror, making it obvious she did.

"Fantino is fine. He's awake in another room. Maybe now you're awake, you can be moved from ICU to join him."

"That's for the doctor to decide." A nurse came in and approached the bed. "It's good to see you awake, Mrs. Messina." She said to Annette. "We'll need you to leave for the present, but you can come back after she's been assessed by the doctor."

Annette brushed her sister's cheek. "We'll be back. I have some amazing news for you."

Joyce's eyes shifted to something at Annette's left and she realized Carlo was standing there. He must have gone for the nurse when Annette realized Joyce was awake. But he was here now and Joyce was asking silently if he was part of the amazing news.

"Yes, he's part of it," Annette said aloud. "But I'm not telling you more until I come back."

The laughter in Joyce's eyes said she understood Annette was giving her something to look forward to, and also teasing a little, as big sisters did sometimes.

"Fantino is going to be ecstatic that you have woken," Carlo said. "We will go tell him."

Joyce's relaxed expression said that was all she needed to hear right now.

Carlo and Annette left the room, but ran into Lynette as she was coming back.

Carlo put his arm out. "The doctors want a chance to assess your sister and hopefully remove the tubes that are preventing her speech."

Lynnette nodded and then just fell on Annette. "She's all right. I didn't think she would be."

Annette let their oldest sister cry, even as she stood in stunned silence that Lynette would choose her as a point of comfort. It ended as abruptly as it began as soon as their parents voices could be heard in the corridor.

Lynette broke from Annette and ran for them.

They stood together, a tableau of three, no room for her.

Carlo once again slid his arm around her, pulling her into his body. "Come, we have an appointment to keep and then we will return and share our good news with your sister."

Annette was nervous going into her appointment, still bothered by the fact it had never even occurred to her she might be pregnant. The youth in her program would be laughing their heads off at her if they knew. However, the doctor was kind with an approachable manner.

"We could do another urine test to confirm your pregnancy, but as we would then perform an ultrasound, we might as well start there, with the added benefit of not emptying your bladder."

So, there was a reason the office had instructed her to drink at least four cups of water an hour before her ultrasound. And it wasn't just to leave her with an urgent need for the restroom.

Laying on the exam table a few minutes later, naked from the waist down and her stomach covered in cold gel, Annette wasn't prepared for what she saw on the monitor. "I can see their little mouth and eyes."

"It is our baby," Carlo said, his own voice heavy with suppressed emotion.

"Yes, and our measurements match your calculations. You are four months pregnant."

"She's not showing though. Should we be worried?" Carlo asked.

The doctor gave him a look that said *new fathers, what can you do?* "There's nothing to worry about at all. The baby's size is commensurate with being eighteen weeks along. Some women show early, some quite late."

They were given a thumb drive with the ultrasound pictures on it and instructions for foods to avoid during pregnancy. Thankfully none of which she'd been indulging in since returning from Sicily.

"You haven't been drinking coffee?" Carlo asked with surprise as they walked out to the car waiting for them at the curb.

"It made me nauseated. I thought I was getting a stress ulcer, to tell you the truth."

"Because of your worry about Joyce?" he asked, his dark brow furrowed.

"That was only part of it. I told you what was going on in the organization and all that I had uncovered since becoming a regional director. Knowing how I'd supported and worked for an organization that didn't practice the core values it claimed to uphold was soul destroying."

"Were my legal staff not able to help?"

"Oh, they're helping the employees I got them in touch with, but that didn't change my own sense of personal responsibility."

"You take too much on yourself."

"You think so?"

"You blamed yourself for the accident."

"My parents did too."

He frowned. "If anything, they should be grateful, as we are, that you were willing to step in and help your sister and Fantino when the rest of us ignored what was happening, telling ourselves it was just part of being new parents."

"You really feel that way?" she asked.

"*Sì*. So do my parents. We are all very grateful to you, just as Fantino is."

Warmth unfurled inside Annette. He and his family appreciated her and it felt good.

As nice as that was, by the time they had visited with Joyce and Fantino again, sharing their good news with her sister, Annette was exhausted and ready for dinner and an early night.

Chapter Fourteen

The next morning, Annette woke with a complete sense of wellbeing.

She remembered the last time that had happened and what had come after. The prick of that memory threatened to burst the sense of contentment surrounding her.

Warm breath exhaled over her temple and Annette smiled. Not the same.

Carlo was beside her in the bed, his body wrapped around hers, his hand settled over her lower abdomen even in his sleep. Carlo really wanted this baby, and Annette really wanted a family. With him. That bit was something she had to come to terms with for her own sense of equanimity.

Both Joyce and Fantino were awake now, and soon enough Jo-Jo was going to have her own family back. The six-month-old would not need her aunt like she did now, but the baby growing inside Annette would always need her. She could love that child without telling herself not to get too attached, to remember she was not the mom.

But this baby had a father too, one very keen to shower his child with love and affection, protection, and care.

Annette didn't know if her biological father had felt that way at one time about her, but whatever feelings he had for her died with her mother, she was sure of that. Could Carlo get turned off his own child that easily?

She didn't think so, but how could she know?

Carlo stirred, his hand rubbing a slow circle over her belly before leaning down to kiss her neck and then shifting so they were face to face. "You look thoughtful," he said.

"So, no big wedding?" she asked, rather than ask a question sure to offend him.

"Are you saying there is going to be a wedding at all?"

"You haven't actually asked me."

"I did that five years ago." And his tone said, *look where that got us*.

She had to acknowledge he had a point. "So, *if* there is a wedding, no church?" she rephrased her question.

"No." That was definite.

But then he probably had very bad memories of standing in the front of a full church only to have a no-show bride.

She nodded. "Good."

"You did not want a church wedding before?" he asked, clearly surprised.

"I didn't want a spectacle." She'd hated the thought of saying their vows in front of hundreds of people that were strangers to her.

"You did not say."

"My mother took over planning the wedding practically from the moment I told my parents that we were getting married."

"Surely she wanted your opinion on things."

"Trust me, she didn't."

"A celebrant and only the necessary witnesses," Carlo said. "Perhaps in our sibling's shared hospital room."

If all went well, the doctors thought Joyce would be able to be moved into Fantino's room before the end of the week. Alceu was already looking into what it would take to bring them both home soonest so they could see their baby and Fantino could get his physical therapy in familiar surroundings.

"You want to get married this week?" she asked with an embarrassingly shocked squeak in her voice.

"You heard Fantino, you do not need the stress of a wedding late in your pregnancy."

And maybe he thought that if they didn't put it off too long, she was more likely to follow through.

"If we get married, we already agreed there will be no big production. Therefore, no stress."

Frowning, Carlo nevertheless nodded. He withdrew from her, though, and got out of bed.

"Carlo?"

"I have some work to attend to this morning. I cannot keep putting off my responsibilities."

"Visiting your brother is part of those responsibilities, isn't it?"

"*Sì.* Even so..." He shrugged, grabbed his slacks and slid them on before heading to the door, the rest of his clothes in hand.

Something had happened there and Annette wasn't sure what it was. "Carlo. Stop. What is going on?"

"I have work. I said."

"Yes, you did. I just..."

"What?" He turned to face her. "You think my pride likes the constant reminders that I'm good enough for sex, but not good enough for marriage as far you are concerned?"

"I never said that!"

"You have said it in too many ways to count, but jilting me at the altar was the biggest one."

"I didn't jilt you at the altar. I jilted you to your face, but you were too arrogant to believe I meant what I said."

"Arrogant? Trusting you to mean what you said was arrogant?"

"I meant it when I said the wedding was off."

He ran his hands through his hair. "Why? Why was it off?"

"Do you remember saying my job was an embarrassment to you?"

"*Sì.* That was unacceptable, but you do run away from your own wedding because your groom says one foolish thing?"

"Even if you meant it?"

"I was arrogant about that, I admit it. I had ideas, this picture in my head of what a perfect family would be like."

"And in that family, I didn't have a job." She scooted up in the bed, making no attempt to hide her nudity.

His grey eyes flared with interest, but then he met her gaze, his expression almost contrite. "That was wrong of me."

Not almost. He was sorry. Good. Maybe there was hope for them yet.

She nodded. "It was, but it wasn't just that."

"What else?"

"I had this feeling, like I could never measure up to the perfect wife you wanted me to be, and I'd spend my whole life trying to be perfect and never being able to earn my family's love."

"So, you thought I would eventually treat you like they do?" he asked, clearly appalled at the idea, and also offended. "I would not have done that. You were, and are again, precious to me."

She about melted on the spot, but precious wasn't the same as loving. "I wanted you to love me. I thought maybe you did, only then you made all those plans without even talking to me and I knew you couldn't, could you?"

"Love?" He shook his head, letting out a sigh. "I'm not a romantic. Not like my father and brother."

Right. That's what she'd finally realized. "But you wanted to marry me. Why?"

"We fit. In bed and out of it, or so I thought."

"I did too. Until I didn't."

"Until you did not." He sighed again. "I guess you need to take some time and decide if you think we can fit again."

"I thought you were going to try to persuade me."

"I make no promises not to do that, but for now, I think we both deserve time to think."

She nodded. He was right. Of course, he was right.

So, why did him leaving her room like this feel so wrong?

Annette found the next week odd and if she were honest with herself, trying.

She and Carlo were living in the same house, but he'd started sleeping in his own guest room. They ate breakfast together every morning, though he had to interrupt his already busy workday to do so. He also joined her and Jo-Jo on their daily walk.

Both of which showed his commitment to spending time with her and their niece, but the intimacy they had shared even while at odds was gone.

They talked about Joyce and Fantino, the business, and even Annette's job and what she might want to do going forward. They did not talk about their relationship and the topic of marriage was not brought up again between them. Annette was afraid Carlo had changed his mind and was interested in shared custody rather than a shared life.

She had no idea what her Sicilian lover was really thinking, though.

They'd finally cleared the air about their failed attempt to marry the first time and yet Annette felt like they were further apart than ever in some ways.

Carlo was unfailingly polite, but he did not touch her. At all.

She missed his touches and wasn't ashamed to say so. To herself. Alone. In her room when she was missing them most and trying to sleep, but often failing miserably.

The night before Fantino was supposed to return home, Annette fell asleep when her head hit the pillow from pure exhaustion, only to waken in a cold sweat sometime later, the echo of nightmares she could not remember reverberating through her consciousness. She didn't remember the dreams, but she remembered the sense of loss.

Knowing she would not get back to sleep right away, she got up. Maybe a cup of chamomile tea would help. She shivered and grabbed her robe. She pulled it on over her pajamas. She'd taken to wearing a long-sleeved t-shirt and flannel sleep pants the last couple of nights because she'd been cold in her bed. She missed Carlo's body radiating heat.

There was a light under the door into the kitchen when she reached it.

Pushing open the door, she was unsurprised to find Carlo sitting at the table, drinking a mug of something. The kitchen was dimly lit from the light over the stove, the overhead lights not on.

"I hope that's not coffee. You'll never get any sleep if it is."

His head jerked up like he hadn't heard her come in. "Oh, uh...no." He grimaced. "I'm embarrassed to say it is warm milk with vanilla and sugar like my mother used to make when I couldn't sleep as a boy."

"Sounds yummy, though I don't know how the sugar was supposed to help you sleep."

He shrugged. "It always worked back then."

"Maybe I should try it then."

He stood. "Sit down, I will make you some."

"You don't have to do that. I'm sure I can figure it out."

"Sit, Annette. You look as drawn out as when I first arrived. And we had good news today."

"Yes, Fantino is coming home and if this last infection stays gone, Joyce gets to come home in a few days."

"She will need help."

"Yes." And while Jo-Jo transitioned to bonding with her mother, that help needed to be Annette, but not for too long. She needed to leave so the family could find its footing together again.

Without her.

Carlo moved around the kitchen with surprising efficiency, preparing her a cup of warmed milk in a saucepan, not the microwave as she would have done. He handed her the steaming mug and then returned to his own seat and proceeded to stare at his own cup like it held the secrets of the universe.

"Is something the matter?" she asked after several seconds of silence.

He looked up, again like he was almost startled to find her there. "Drink your milk while it's warm or it won't do you any good."

"Really?" She took a sip and the flavor of vanilla slid across her tongue. "Mmm...yum. I wonder why it matters if it is warm."

"Warmth and comfort, I guess. I do not know. It is something my mother used to say to me."

"Valentina was a good mom."

"*Sì*. She was, but for many years I did not think so. I thought she neglected me and my brother, because she was not the one to come to our football matches, or volunteer at school like the other mothers."

"She didn't neglect you though, did she?" Valentina had always had her causes, but she loved her family.

"Not really, no." He frowned. "When I was young, I resented the time she spent on her causes, her many trips away to service them. We always had nannies, and our grandparents were active in our lives, but Fantino and I both felt badly that our mother was rarely around for the things that mattered to us."

"I am sorry. If she knew she hurt you, she would be sorry for it."

"She was a wonderful mother," he said, like he'd come to the conclusion long before. "Her life was about more than my brother and I and she has done so much good."

"But when you were a child, you wanted her to be like the other moms."

"*Sì*. Now, I appreciate the woman she is."

"But that's why my job was such a problem for you. You saw my dedication to at risk youth as a competition for dedication to our own family."

"We didn't even have children yet, and yes I know I tried to guilt you into having them earlier than we planned. I've done a lot of thinking this past week and I ask myself if I set out to break us up because my actions couldn't have ended with any other scenario."

"Do you think you wanted out of the marriage, but didn't want to break your word?" she asked, pain at the idea a solid lump in her chest.

He shook his head decisively and then met her gaze, his own intent. "No. I think I was what you accused me of being. Arrogant. I believed that because you were so malleable with your family, you would be malleable with me when it mattered. Or when I thought it mattered. My entire life, I have found it easier to ask pardon than to ask permission. And so, I did what I always had done, made my plans and then told you about them after the fact, assuming that even if you were angry, you would get over it."

"And you would get your way." She took another sip of her warmed milk, finding it comforting but his willingness to talk even more so.

He nodded, looking chagrined. "In no scenario did I actually expect you to dump me."

"You were very sure of me."

"You told me you loved me."

"You said you aren't a romantic."

"I am not. I am pragmatic and I thought if you loved me, then so much the better."

"How did that work out for you?" she asked with only a little sarcasm.

"As you know, it did not work at all."

"And now?"

He came around the table, dropping to his knees beside her chair and taking both her hands in his. "Now? Now, I must tell you how very sorry I am for taking you for granted, for treating you like you were not the most precious person in my life as you were. I should never have planned that honeymoon, hoping to get you to quit your job. That was inexcusable, and I paid dearly for my arrogance."

He considered losing her a dear price to pay?

He kissed her knuckles, and then looked into her eyes, his shining with sincerity and something she'd never seen before in them. Humility. "I am so sorry I made the decision to move back to Sicily without talking to you first. When I told my father, he was livid with me. Said he'd raised me better."

"It shocked me."

"No matter what happens between us going forward, you have my word I will never attempt to manipulate you like that again."

She went to draw her hands away, but he held tight. "I'm not done."

Chapter Fifteen

"There's more?" she asked.

"I have not yet said how much I regret not listening to you that day. You would not be you if you did not want to help others. Your heart is too big to keep it caged in a Sicilian mansion."

"You're positively poetic."

"I am not trying to be."

She smiled. "I believe you. Neither of us is the same person we were five years ago."

"No, we are not." He gave her a slashing grin, some of his usual confidence shining through. "I think now, you would make me listen."

"Yes." She so would.

"But I would not make the same choices either."

"No, I don't think you would." He'd grown, just as she had. That very heartfelt apology showed it. "Just like you didn't with Jo-Jo. You listened to me about her."

"I'm glad you realize that and don't hold the contract against me. That was such a—"

She interrupted before he could start self-flagellating. She was glad he was sorry, but she didn't want him being so down on himself. "You burned it." She'd seen the ashes in the study fireplace. "You never had any intention of forcing me to sign it."

"No. I promise you; I never did."

Since she'd never thought he was serious and it was his version of going off the rails, like he'd said at the hospital, she believed him.

He let go of her hands and stood up. "Now, I do not know what you want." It was a big admission for such a confident, take-charge man.

"I want a family," Annette assured him. "But I want to work and make a difference for at risk youth too."

"*Sì*. Absolutely. You would not be the precious woman that you are otherwise. I finally understand that."

"It's only taken five years." Which really? Wasn't all that long in the scheme of things.

He smiled. "You always take the positive view."

"I didn't five years ago," she admitted.

"You were wrong about one thing."

"What's that?"

He reached down and grabbed his mug, drinking what appeared to be the last of his warmed milk and then put the mug down. "I didn't need a perfect wife. I wanted you. I still want you."

"Even though I'm a bad bet?" she teased.

"You are not. Neither am I, because I will never again make choices for you without consulting you, this I promise you."

"There are other deal breakers, but that's a big one."

"Oh, yes, what are they?" He got up and put both now empty mugs in the sink.

She stood, yawning, suddenly very tired. "I'll put them in the prenup."

He went very still. "You are saying you will marry me?"

"Yes, Carlo, I will marry you. This time we both have a better understanding of what we expect going in."

"We do, but there will be no prenup."

"What?" Even the shock of that statement couldn't rouse much energy in her. "Did you put sleeping pills in my milk?"

"No, you are just worn out worrying about everyone. It cannot be good for you, or the baby."

"No, I don't suppose it is." She covered her mouth before yawning again.

He guided her from the kitchen, his arm at her back all the way up the stairs and down the hall to her room.

She stopped in front of her door, but didn't go in. "Sleep with me. I'm cold without you."

Carlo didn't reply but he followed her into her room.

The next morning Annette met Carlo for breakfast like usual. What was not usual was the ring box sitting beside her plate.

It was the same jeweler that had done her engagement ring before. "Is that?"

"Your engagement ring? *Sì*. It has been sitting in my safe since your father returned it to me." He shook his head. "I thought that told me how little regard you had for it. You didn't want me or the ring I'd had custom made for you, but the expression on your lovely features says the opposite."

"I love that ring." But she'd felt wrong keeping it after calling off the wedding.

Carlo opened the box and took out the ring. Annette offered her hand and he slid the ring on her finger. It was déjà vu and not. They'd done this once before, but this time, Annette knew they were getting married to build a family.

She wasn't building castles in the sky around love and happily ever after.

They would be good together if they were good to each other.

She loved him and had every intention of being the best human in his life she could be. Annette trusted that Carlo was just as determined. He'd grown in the past five years, just as she had.

Smiling she sat down to the table, thrilled to see her favorite smoked salmon and gouda omelet on her plate. There was fruit and toast as well, but she ignored both to take and then savor a bite of the omelet, making *mmm* noises.

"You know some doctors claim cravings are your body's way of getting the nourishment it needs," Carlo said with a smile. "Have you had your iron levels checked recently?"

"I'm sure it was included in the panel the obstetrician had run." They'd taken two vials of blood after all. "The nurse said everything came back normal when she called."

"I'd feel better if you checked your health chart app."

"Fine. After breakfast. Right now, I'm going to eat this yummy omelet before it goes cold."

"A very prosaic way to celebrate our engagement, but not a bad one."

She grinned at him. "I can't drink champagne, but I can eat fish."

"Not too much fish. Some studies—"

"Shh...after breakfast."

He dutifully went silent, making a sign of zipping his lips. However, Annette had no doubts he'd be having a talk with Mrs. Banning about how much fish should be served at meals in future.

"I am still the President of Messina Shipping and Exports," Carlo said as they finished their meal.

"Yes, I know."

"It is possible we could move my offices to New York."

Touched at the proof that he was not taking anything for granted this time around, Annette shook her head. "Not necessary. I'm not staying with my organization so now is as good a time as any to make the move to Sicily. I speak Italian and can look for a job over there, but honestly after the past few months, I'd like to take some time to regroup. Maybe a sabbatical at least until after our baby is born and we see how mundane things like breast feeding and sleeping through the night go for us."

"If that is what you truly want?" He wasn't being diffident. There was too much quiet confidence in his demeanor, but he was taking nothing for granted this time around. She approved.

"I do."

"That will make my next request an easier one to make then."

"Yes?" she inquired.

"I hoped you would be willing to wait to look for another position until after our honeymoon."

"We're going on a honeymoon?" For a marriage of convenience because they liked having sex and didn't seem inclined to stop doing it together and she'd gotten pregnant as a result?

"It is customary."

"All right, but I want to give Joyce, Fantino and Jo-Jo a few days to settle in after Joyce comes home, before I leave."

"Naturally. It will be hard on both you and Jo-Jo when you leave, but if she is going to bond with her mother..." He let his voice trail off and shrugged.

"She has to see Joyce as mommy and not Aunt Annette. I know." Emotion washed over her. Worry and doubt and fear a maelstrom that always seemed ready to take over.

And it made no sense because Joyce and Fantino were improving every day.

"I just wish I knew how to make it easier on all of them," she told Carlo.

"You take too much on yourself, but I have been making plans."

"You have?"

He just looked at her.

She almost laughed, but was afraid she'd start crying if she did. Darn hormones. "Of course, you have. What are they?"

"I've spoken to the clinic she went to, and they are sending a psychologist who specializes in adoption transitions to facilitate those first weeks with Joyce home."

Relief washed through Annette. It wasn't on her to fix it this time. Someone who knew what they were doing was going to guide Joyce and Fantino. "Jo-Jo isn't adopted though," she couldn't help pointing out, nevertheless.

"No, but many things about the situation have a similar emotional makeup, or so the director for the clinic claimed."

That made sense, Annette supposed. Joyce and Jo-Jo's bond was tenuous at best. While Jo-Jo seemed happy for Fantino to hold her and play with her, she still reached for Annette when she needed comfort. That had to change for the baby's sake and her parents' sakes.

"My parents will remain in New York for the next few months. My father will cover Fantino's office until my brother is able to return to work fulltime."

"Aren't you worried for his health?" The senior Messina had recovered from his accident, but he was in his seventies now and she worried the stress of working the long work hours he and his sons were known for could be detrimental.

"No," Carlo said with assurance. "Mama will be policing his time and she can be a dragon if she needs to."

Annette agreed. She thought Valentina Messina was a formidable woman even when she didn't need to be, but she was also very occupied with her own projects. "Will she be able to keep track of Alceu's hours when she herself is so busy?"

"Mama has slowed down her involvements since Papa retired. They spend more time together. They travel a great deal."

"Oh, that's good then."

"I have also used my time here in New York to identify additional members of management staff who will make solid adds to Fantino's executive team. He approved my choices this morning and I have had human resources contact each with their promotion offers. This will free up more experienced executive team members to take some of the daily burden from my father."

"You're a good son."

Carlo looked pleased with her assessment, and it occurred to Annette that he'd always liked praise from her when he seemed indifferent to it from everyone else. Except his family.

Further proof that in his mind she was on equal footing with his family, which was not a bad place to be in the life of the Sicilian tycoon.

Fantino came home that evening and Joyce five days later. The psychologist from California arrived at the same time. He fit right in with the household, insisting on being called Ray and began facilitating the adjustment of the little family toward what would be *their* normal almost immediately.

Annette and Carlo were out walking together with Jo-Jo, since neither parent could manage the task just yet, when Carlo said, "Ray is a good man and competent doctor, I am sure, but I am glad I am not Fantino right now."

"Because you'd have to talk about your *feelings* at least daily?" she teased.

But Carlo nodded quickly, his look of utter horror at the prospect making her laugh.

"Feelings don't make you weak, Carlo."

"Nor does talking about them make them any more real," he countered.

But Annette wasn't sure she agreed. "Maybe it does."

"No. All this talking, it brings up more bad than good."

"At first, maybe, but not talking about it doesn't mean the bad wasn't there, under the surface."

"You think they have a bad marriage?" he asked, sounding shocked.

"I didn't say that. You're the one that used the term bad. I would say difficult. Joyce and Fantino stopped communicating during her depression and now they have to find their way back to each other and being able to freely share their hearts and ideas once again."

"We are open with each other." Carlo took over the stroller as they started up a muddy, steep track. Annette had slid backwards on this before and he wouldn't risk her falling.

She walked beside him. "Yes, we are, but we weren't always."

"That is true," he admitted, his tone grudging. "We didn't need a psychologist to get us to open up this time though."

"Speak for yourself. I was in therapy for three years after I moved to Portland."

He didn't reply. She cast him a sidelong glance and found him looking back, his expression questioning. "It helped?"

"It helped."

"I am glad."

She was too, but that wasn't what she wanted to talk about. They'd set a wedding date, one week from today, after which, they planned to go on the long-delayed honeymoon. They'd agreed on who should be invited to the wedding.

Annette had thought long and hard and finally decided against inviting anyone in her family except Joyce. It was her wedding day and while she wasn't marrying her Knight in Shining Armor who loved her to pieces like she'd always dreamed, it was still special.

Annette loved Carlo. Deeply and forever.

She wanted nothing but goodwill on her wedding day and she was certain that if she invited her older sister and her parents, that would not be her experience.

One thing she'd definitely gotten out of therapy was that she was not responsible for the actions of others. If her parents were toxic to her, even if they were good to their other children, Annette did not have to give them room in *her* life's special moments.

Whether she would give them space in her child's life was something she would decide based on their behavior.

She'd told Carlo as much and he had agreed, but hadn't been happy. He wanted to cut off all ties with her parents for their past treatment of her, but Annette wasn't willing to go that far. For one thing, she knew it would strain her relationship with Joyce and that bond was too important to Annette to harm unless she had no other choice.

None of that was what was on her mind uppermost today though. "Carlo, we haven't signed the prenuptial agreement yet. You know I have a clause or two I want to put in."

"I told you, there will be no prenuptial agreement."

"But why not? I signed one last time."

"And you walked away. This time we are doing things differently."

"But you're a billionaire. You can't just marry me without a prenup." She'd been raised by Floyd Hudson, if not with affection, with all the same strictures her sisters had been taught.

And one of those was to always have a prenuptial agreement to protect their assets. Annette had no assets to speak of, but Carlo had a business empire.

When Carlo remained silent, she asked, "What does your father think about it?"

"He has asked me to sign over my shares in the company to him to protect Messina Shipping and Exports."

"What? No. You've nearly doubled the size of the company since you took it over." The workaholic that he was. "That's not fair."

"I would still draw a more than adequate salary. And I have my own firm."

The venture capital firm he'd created as a young man in business school was now one of the world's leading ones.

"No, I won't let you do it. You tell your father we're signing a contract."

"Fine, if you want one, you work with the lawyers and my father and draw it up, but I warn you that if you try to shortchange yourself somehow, I won't be signing it."

"Why? What is this really about?"

He stopped the stroller at the top of the hill and turned to face her while Jo-Jo babbled at her favorite view. There were cows in the distance and sometimes people walking. The baby seemed to love this vantage point.

Carlo brushed Annette's cheek, the soft leather of his glove making her shiver a little. "This is about making a lifetime commitment to build a family. You are agreeing to it because you are pregnant with my child. That makes it no less real and lasting."

"How does a prenup change that?"

"It gives us a prescription for the way out if things get hard."

"And you don't want that?"

"No. Like anything else worth having, I want to work for our marriage, in the good times, but also the difficult ones."

"You say you are not a romantic." Annette's voice was clogged with emotion. Darn hormones again.

"I am not, but even I recognize that marriage is not a business contract."

"Last time..."

"I did everything expected."

"I still don't see why that is bad."

"It wasn't." Left unsaid was a truth between them: but it hadn't worked.

And in Carlo's mind, it wasn't enough to change how he handled decisions about their lives together, he had to change everything leading up to the wedding.

"You can be a little irrational," she pointed out.

"I am perfectly rational," he said, affronted.

Said the man who had written up that ludicrous sex contract.

"Okay. I will draft the prenup, but don't come whining to me if you don't like some of the clauses."

"I assure you, I will not."

Chapter Sixteen

Chapter 16

He was singing a different tune two days later.

Annette, Alceu and Valentina had pounded out a prenup that satisfied Alceu for the safety of the Messina empire, Valentina about her son's future fatherhood in the event the marriage did not last and Annette about how that marriage and their family life would be conducted.

"You have put limits on the number of hours I may work and how often I can leave the family for business trips."

"There are also limits on the number of trips you can expect us to take each year with you for the sake of business," Annette agreed serenely. "You'll notice there is also a limit on the number of hours I spend working, or volunteering."

She'd put a forty-hour cap on hers because honestly, Annette had always wanted to work only part time when her children were in school, but she didn't want to work extra hours later either. She wanted balance in life.

Carlo's sixty-hour max was generous on her part, but she didn't think the tycoon would countenance any less. However, there were other family centric provisos. Like both of them attending their children's events at least half of the time. Annette had every intention of being there for everything she could, but she expected Carlo to make an effort too.

"It is not reasonable to expect me to make a football match in the middle of my workday, or go to every dance recital."

"It's only half, not every, and why not? You know what I never heard you say when you were talking about the resentments you held toward your mother for not being there when you wanted her?"

"What?" Carlo asked, warily.

"Any resentment toward your father for missing *all* of them."

Arrested, Carlo stared at her. "I...he was running the company."

"A global concern, I know, but he could have delegated more."

"Not without risk."

"Life is made up of risks. You choose which ones you want to take."

"You want me to risk my company for the sake of time with our child?"

"Hopefully children, but yes." He'd been willing to risk the whole she-bang by marrying her without a prenup. It shouldn't be a big stretch.

"You want more than one child?"

"You know I do." Five years ago, they'd agreed on at least two children, but she had always wanted four. So, there was no middle child to be lost on her own.

"I did not know if your desires in that regard had changed."

"A good conversation to have *before* marriage."

He shrugged. "Perhaps, but ultimately, whether we agreed on how many children to have did not matter. You *are* pregnant with our child. We are getting married. If you choose never to get pregnant again, that will not change those basic facts."

"I still think being on the same page about expectation in that regard is nice."

"Certainly, but life does not afford us the luxury of always being on the same page as the people most important to us."

"Is this about your father?" She knew it had hurt Carlo when Alceu had asked him to sign over the shares to the company.

The prenup had allowed Alceu to withdraw the request, but she knew it still rankled with Carlo that the older man had made it.

Carlo shrugged. "It does not matter. My point is that *nice* is not always our luxury."

Since she could not argue with that, Annette didn't try. "He still thinks the world of you, you know?"

Carlo looked at her, the contract pages spread out between them over the library table. Although library was a misnomer. There were books in the room and lots of bookshelves, but they held more objects d'art than reading material.

Joyce was not the reader that Annette was. Apparently, neither was Fantino.

Still, it made a nice room to have this meeting in, having a door that shut snugly with a lock. With his parents staying and both Joyce and Fantino back in residence, along with the psychologist, privacy in the mansion was in short supply.

"I know my father respects me. Do not worry about my tender feelings, Annette. I am fine. It was business and that is one thing I understand very well."

"If you say so." She still wasn't convinced. Something was bothering Carlo and she was certain it was his father's apparent lack of faith in him.

This contract negated all the older Messina man's worries though, so Annette felt good about that. She didn't want father and son at odds. The family had been through enough.

Carlo finished reading the last page and then signed the prenuptial agreement with a flourish. "So, it is done."

"Just like that?" she asked, a little shocked. "I expected some push back and to have to negotiate the number of weeks of vacation time each year at the very least." She'd stipulated six. Two weeks at the winter holidays and four more weeks throughout the year.

She would prefer they were taken in at least weeklong clumps, but she would settle for lots of long weekends so long as he made real time in his schedule to spend with her and their children regularly.

He seemed perfectly willing to do just that.

"I give my top executives six weeks of vacation and an additional two of personal leave. I cannot justify giving myself any less to spend with my own family." Carlo stood, his smile filled with something he usually reserved for the nighttime when they were alone. "I think that sofa looks quite comfortable. Would you like to join me on it?"

He was talking about a large brown leather sofa situated in front of another gas fireplace. It was blocked from the windows by standing bookcases behind it.

She darted a glance to the door.

"I locked it on the way in."

"You were planning this then?" she asked with laughter as she got up and did as he asked, joining him on the sofa.

"I was planning privacy. Now, I want to celebrate."

"Celebrate?"

"Oh, yes. That contract has us both stitched up tight."

"You liked that clause then?"

"Can you doubt it?" he was stripping methodically all the while watching her do the same.

She'd put a clause in that was her solemn promise to show up for the ceremony. She thought a businessman like him would appreciate her putting it in writing. He really did, it looked like.

An hour later, his suitcoat (which they'd used to protect the couch) would never be the same and Annette was left in no doubt just how enthusiastically her tycoon fiancé felt about the prenuptial contract he had just signed.

Annette woke on her wedding day feeling more anticipation than she thought she should. She *should* be worried, but she wasn't. She was excited.

Today, she started building the family she had always craved.

Five years ago, she'd run from Carlo, out of fear of not being enough, and of quite honestly losing herself. She wasn't worried about that now. Carlo had promised he would never try to manipulate her into a big life change again, nor would he make choices that affected her without her input and buy-in. She trusted him to keep his word.

Equally important, Annette was no wilting flower. She could and would hold her own with the billionaire businessman.

Carlo might not be her Prince Charming, and head over heels in love with her, but she'd stopped believing in fairytales, so that was okay.

He was honorable and he believed entirely in the importance of family. He was willing to give what his own father had not. Carlo had promised his time to Annette and their unborn child, and to any other children they might have.

Maybe there was just a tiny bit of Prince Charming in him after all. At the very least that Knight in Shining Armor.

Annette's hand slid down to rest over belly. Their baby. Her family.

All of Carlo's actions to this point indicated a man intent on making a real go of their marriage. Annette couldn't ask for any more than that. Suddenly she felt a movement inside. The baby. She'd felt the baby move! She shifted, hoping it would happen again.

It did.

She was laying there, happiness just bubbling through her when a knock sounded on the door and Annette sat up. "Who is it?"

That hadn't been Carlo's usual knock and besides his mother had threatened him with dire consequences if he tried to see Annette before the wedding. Which meant she had slept alone the night before, but it had been surprisingly soundly.

"It is me, Valentina," her soon to be mother-in-law said through the door.

Annette jumped out of bed and grabbed her robe, calling, "Come in."

Valentina pushed open the door, a sweet smile on her face. "Happy wedding day, Annette."

"What is that?" Annette pointed to a pile of ivory silk shimmering with crystal beading, foaming over Valentina's arms.

Valentina walked forward and laid out the most exquisite antique gown. It had copious crystal beading in an art deco design. "This was my great grandmother's wedding gown."

Annette reached out and touched the embroidered silk. "It looks like it's from the 1920s."

"It is. My great grandparents married in 1927."

"Oh. It's beautiful."

"I've always thought so."

"If it fits," Annette couldn't help offering the caveat because she was a curvy five-foot-three. "I will be honored to wear it."

Not drop waisted but designed like a 1920s evening gown Clara Bow might have worn, the dress fit like it had been made for Annette, hugging her breasts and hips and the beading design accentuating her waist. Valentina had bought shoes in Annette's size to match it, 1920's inspired heels with a t-strap. She had also managed to find a veil with an art deco styled jeweled circlet that could have been made in tandem with the dress.

Joyce joined them with Mrs. Banning in tow, a laden breakfast tray in her hands. All four women found somewhere to sit in Annette's room and ate.

Joyce rested on the bed, her expression as happy as on her own wedding day. "Oh, Annette, I'm so glad you and Carlo found your way back to each other. You two are soulmates and I think the universe would be really mad if you hadn't."

Annette laughed and shook her head but left her younger sister to her romantic fantasies. Soulmates or not, she was marrying the love of her life and that had to be enough.

Annette looked in the mirror ninety minutes later and felt tears tighten her throat.

"Don't you dare cry and mess up your makeup," Joyce warned her. "You'll ruin all of Valentina's efforts and start your marriage on the wrong side of our mother-in-law."

All three women laughed as did Mrs. Banning and the stylist Valentina had brought in to do all their hair and the other women's makeup.

Valentina had insisted on doing Annette's makeup herself though. She'd done the same with Joyce, despite their mother's protest. Valentina really was a formidable woman when she wanted to be. And continuing family tradition brought it out in her.

"I'm just...it's..." Annette shook her head.

"It is your wedding day. You are overcome with emotion," Valentina said complacently. "It is as it should be."

"Exactly as it should be," Joyce agreed.

Alceu met the women at the top of the stairs and surprised Annette by putting his arm out to escort her, and not his wife.

He walked her down the stairs and to the formal living room in the Upstate New York mansion. Decorated in a more formal style than the rest of the house, it would have made a pretty setting for the ceremony to come without all the gorgeous winter floral arrangements giving the space a festive air.

Annette did not know who was responsible for the flowers, but she was grateful. She hadn't wanted a spectacle, but it *was* her wedding, and they gave the ambiance that took from convenience for the sake of an accidental pregnancy to something more.

Looking gorgeous in a dark bespoke tuxedo with short waist and tails, Carlo stood with a judge who had been chosen to officiate near the large, ornate fireplace.

Fantino sat in a wheelchair beside Carlo, his broken leg raised as it was supposed to be. Alceu leaned in to kiss Annette's cheek before stepping back and leading his wife to a white Queen Anne style sofa, where they sat down together. Pamina sat in a matching armchair, with Jo-Jo, who had been provided a frothy lace dress for the occasion in her lap.

Joyce took her spot beside Annette, as it was supposed to be.

Only one other person was in the room: a professional photographer. It was a private ceremony for a private event, but there would be pictures to put out with the press release.

Annette met Carlo's gaze as she crossed the floor toward him. His grey eyes were almost black, his face inscrutable, like he was intent on not letting any emotion show through. However, the heat in his gaze could be felt across the expanse of the large room.

That warmth gave her feet the impetus to move. She could do this.

When she reached him, he handed her a beautiful bouquet of crimson roses mixed with white star lilies and baby's breath. It was the bouquet she'd wanted five years ago and been vetoed by her mother, who had wanted pastels.

Annette's gaze flew to his. She was touched and she let him see that in her expression. Carlo smiled, the pleasure at her approval seeping through the emotionless façade.

"Thank you," she said, her voice low.

Carlo nodded. "It is my pleasure."

She saw the flowers around the room with new eyes. They were all in the same festive, red and white theme. Suddenly she knew Carlo had ordered them and no one else.

Yes, maybe there *was* a bit of Prince Charming in the man she was marrying.

The ceremony was brief, but they both spoke vows they technically did not have to. The judge could have signed off on the marriage without any verbal promises being made.

She and Carlo had agreed that they *wanted* to make verbal promises. And so they did.

Vows of fidelity, honesty, respect, and to live together for as long as they were both alive. The weight of those promises hit Annette much harder than she expected.

The kiss took Annette by surprise. They hadn't talked about including *that*. However, she responded immediately, allowing her lips to part and soften under his.

He didn't turn the kiss intimate, but the passion surged between them like an electric current all the same. It probably only lasted a matter of seconds, but Annette felt dizzy, like she'd been holding her breath for a long time.

She swayed a little and Carlo put his arm around her waist to hold her up as everyone in the room took turns congratulated them on their marriage.

Chapter Seventeen

Carlo watched Annette, though he pretended interest in the lively discussion around the table as they shared a family lunch to celebrate the wedding.

He was married.

To the woman he had once thought he *would* marry and later believed to be the one woman he would *never* marry. But when they'd discovered she carried his child, all his determination to get over his sexual obsession with her went by the wayside.

Not that said determination had been bearing much fruit.

He could feel nothing but satisfaction that she had spoken her vows with him today. He understood better now how much those promises meant to her and that her walking away five years ago had not been about breaking her promise to him. She'd been trying to avoid what she was convinced would be a disaster.

Oh, she'd put it differently, but it amounted to the same thing.

Annette had refused to fit into the mold he'd set for her. Not because she did not care about him as he'd made himself believe, but because she simply could not do it. He understood that. How hollow had he felt when his father had asked Carlo to sign those shares over to him?

And it had not meant that Carlo would no longer be President of the company, but he'd still felt like part of him was to be stripped away.

Annette didn't run a multinational corporation, but the work she did with at-risk youth was just as important to her. He would never forget that again.

Nor would he forget all those family time clauses in their prenuptial agreement. Because as important as her work was to her, it was clear that her family would be as well. And she expected their family to be important to him too.

She always made him stop and think in new ways and he hoped she would always care enough to do that.

His father stood up to make a toast. "To my dear son, Carlo, may your marriage be filled with joy and blessed with many children."

Annette smiled, winked and mouthed *four and that's it* to him.

Everyone else read her lips as he did and burst into laughter.

Fantino tapped his glass and made his own toast, followed by Joyce and then his mother.

Carlo was unaccountably touched by the very personal well wishes and realized that he was glad they had not had a big wedding like they'd planned five years ago. This felt so much more real, like a day of promises, not a production put on for the guests.

Carlo lifted his own glass to toast his bride. "It might have taken five years, but we got here in the end."

"When my brother knows what he wants, he doesn't stop going after it," Fantino said with a lift of his own glass.

He sat beside his wife, their daughter in Joyce's lap, the picture of family contentment. They had been through the wars, but they got their happy endings as modern fairytales promised, and Carlo couldn't be happier for them.

Everyone around the table laughed, but Carlo was struck by his brother's words as sure as if they had been a blow. Because he'd wanted Annette five years ago and he'd given up pretty damn easily. What did that say about his supposed stubborn resolve?

Or had he been lying to himself five years ago when he said he'd let her go? How quickly he'd fallen into bed with her after seeing her again gave credence to that theory.

Whatever his past mistakes, he was married to the woman now and his satisfaction was greater than he'd ever before experienced in his life.

He wondered what she would think if she knew? Call him a throwback no doubt, but he couldn't deny it. He was done lying to himself.

Carlo had only ever wanted to marry Annette and now their lives were joined.

A few hours later, they were ensconced in side-by-side seats on his jet, sipping bubbly, though Annette's was of the nonalcoholic variety.

"Where are we going?" she asked him.

Finally.

When he'd asked if she wanted to make the plans for their honeymoon together, she'd told him no. She wanted to be surprised. Like she was intent on erasing the past with new memories.

He was happy to oblige, though she might think he'd taken it too far. "The Dalmatian Coast."

A near identical trip to their aborted honeymoon. However, rather than two months, they had two weeks.

He would have preferred longer, but after everything he had to get back to the office. He would make a concentrated effort in the year to come to build up his own executive team so he could work shorter hours and take more time off.

"In Croatia?" she asked, her tone laced with surprise.

"*Sì.*" She had always wanted to go to Croatia, and particularly the Dalmatian Coast because of the heavy influence from the ancient cultures of Italy and Greece that could be found there. Did she think he had forgotten that?

"I was half afraid you'd never want to vacation in Croatia, or Greece because of the honeymoon that didn't happen."

"That was not going to happen." He'd bought a house there, hadn't he? Not that he'd stayed in it in the past five years, but he hadn't taken a real vacation in that time either. Which brought up something he wanted to say to her. "You are right. I never considered my father's hours at work, or weeks away from home a problem, and yet I begrudged my mother her work in a very childlike fashion, even into my adulthood."

It shamed him to realize the double standard he had entertained for his parents. He was not a product of the last century, but a man of today.

"That's an amazing breakthrough in self-realization," she said with some awe.

Which both irked and pleased him. He liked when she looked at him like that, when her voice took that tone. But she should not be so surprised he could make such strides. "I'm no throwback."

"Are you sure about that?" The obviously teasing glint in her eyes took any sting the words might have had.

"If I am a throwback, you are too." He was thinking of the near primal possessiveness they felt toward each other.

"You might be right. In some ways, anyway." She yawned and then blushed. "Sorry. I don't know why I'm tired. I slept well last night."

"While I barely slept."

"Why?"

"I'll tell you all about it when we reach the Dalmatian Coast house."

"If this jet is anything like the one you had five years ago, it has a bedroom." She gave a near comical waggle of her brows, but then yawned again.

He laughed. "It does and I expect you to use it, but we will not have our first night making love as a married couple in bed on an airplane."

"Why not?"

"Because you, my dear, *pregnant* bride, need your sleep."

He could see she was gearing up to argue, but the third yawn in as many minutes made even his stubborn bride realize she needed rest.

Carlo spent most of the hours of the flight working while his wife slumbered alone in the plane's bedroom.

Carlo roused Annette to prepare for landing and she followed him blearily back into the main cabin, taking her seat and buckling in as the plane began its descent.

They'd arrived in Croatia in the middle of the night, and everything was cast in shadows of darkness as they disembarked the private jet and transferred to a luxury SUV. One bodyguard rode up front with the driver and the rest of the team followed in a second SUV.

Annette had slept on the plane, but she was still tired. She didn't even try to see the countryside out the window in the darkness, but as exhausted as she felt, Annette was also too wired to fall asleep.

Carlo put his phone away after checking something and then tugged, so Annette rested against his chest. Suddenly, that nervous energy keeping her awake just disappeared and she slumped into him, her body going boneless for sleep.

It took only about twenty minutes to reach the house from the private airstrip, but Annette was already dozing against his chest when the SUV pulled to a stop.

Carlo caressed her beautiful, silky blonde hair tenderly. She was exhausted and needed her sleep.

His body was taut with need. It was their wedding night, but he would have to be a monster to try to seduce her into making love in her condition. No matter how much he knew she thought she wanted the same thing.

Stifling his baser urges, he reached down and released the catch on her seatbelt.

Her scent wafted to him, triggering an atavistic response he had no control over. However, while he might not be able to stop himself getting a hardon, he had absolute control over whether he acted on it.

Ignoring his body's need, he cupped her shoulder and shook gently. "Wake up, *bèdda mia*. We are here."

Her eyes fluttered open, their emerald depths warming in recognition. "Carlo."

That was all she said, like his name was a sentence all on its own. It went through him like a lightning bolt, this unfiltered reaction from her.

Giving into one urge, he leant down and swept her up against his chest.

"You're going to carry me over the threshold," she said with sleepy approval.

He was doing just that, so did not think she needed verbal agreement. In fact, he carried her up the stairs to the bedroom he had designated as theirs. It was decorated in the colors she preferred with warm, traditional wood furniture.

He helped her undress and get into the king-sized bed, but Annette did not lay down. She looked ready to fall asleep sitting up.

"Why don't you lie down?" he asked her as he kicked off his shoes.

"I'm waiting."

He shrugged out of his suitcoat and hung it on the wooden rack that had been installed for that purpose. "For what?"

"You," she said like that should have been obvious.

Carlo finished stripping out of his clothes with efficient movements, adding to the pile of hers on the floor. Domestic staff would see to the clothing the next day. Though he did hang the trousers from his bespoke suit over the rail below his jacket.

He climbed into the bed and Annette immediately scooted toward the center. Pulling her into his arms, he settled them against the pillows.

"We aren't going to make love?" she asked in a voice laced with exhaustion.

The obstetrician had warned Annette might need more than her usual amount of sleep. It appeared that possibility had finally caught up with them.

"In the morning."

"Promise?" she asked, snuggling into him like she liked to do.

"*Sì.*"

"Good." She patted his chest and relaxed fully, her breathing going even in sleep only minutes later.

With the feel of his wife's delectable body wrapped snugly against his own, it took Carlo considerably longer to find slumber.

Annette woke feeling fully refreshed and alert. She was feeling something else, too. Desire.

Carlo's arms were tight around her, his big body pressed against hers. She felt protected and cared for, whatever their reason for getting married.

He'd brought her to bed, but he hadn't pushed making love. Annette had been almost completely out of it the night before, she'd been so tired, but she had felt the hardness of his erection against her.

He'd been turned on, but he hadn't tried to seduce her into staying awake to make love.

Nevertheless, she did not think it would bother him if she woke *him* for that purpose.

Annette carefully extracted herself from Carlo's arms and went to use the bathroom. When she returned, she found her husband's steel grey eyes open.

Oh, she did like the sound of that. *Her husband*. She could revel as much as she liked in the privacy of her own heart and mind, too. Though she thought Carlo might be the one person who understood and would not judge her somewhat primitive urges where he was concerned.

Smiling, she rejoined him on the bed. "Good morning." She gave him a heated once over. "I have plans."

"For me?" he asked, desire thick in his voice, and his grey gaze filled with sensual need.

She returned the look with interest. "For us both."

His smile stole her breath, but not her ability to move. She pressed her naked body right up against that of her husband. The man she had always craved and would always love.

He slashed a smile at her. "You look like the cat that got the cream."

"Do I?"

"*Sì*," he growled and then he kissed her, all possessive demand.

She kissed him back the same way, laying claim to the only man she'd ever really wanted to. The kiss went on for minute after minute, while they ate at each other's lips, the slide of his tongue against hers tantalizing and sensual. Their bodies pressed tightly together, his strong arms circling around her, holding her close.

Annette buried her hands in his hair, needing his head to stay just where it was, craving this kiss as she'd never craved another.

Even with him.

They were married. She hadn't thought that would make any difference to this, to sex.

Only, somehow, it did. She felt a confidence that often eluded her, a sense of belonging, a certainty of connection. They hadn't married for love, but her sense of connection with him went to the very core of her soul.

Finally, she could wait no longer to touch him in all the ways she yearned for, and she broke the kiss.

He resisted at first when she wanted to pull away, but then he let her go.

She slid back just a little and smiled at him with a sense of feminine power. "Trust me."

His eyes narrowed, but he nodded his proud Sicilian head nearly imperceptibly.

She smiled again, but then she leaned down and began to kiss along his neck, using her teeth gently to increase the sensation for him.

"*Bèdda mia*," he groaned.

She liked when he called her beautiful. She liked it even more when he added the possessive *mia* to it.

Taking her time, Annette mapped her new husband's body with her mouth and hands, touching him in ways she knew excited him, and taking note of spots heretofore unknown that elicited masculine groans of excitement.

Her body had brushed against his rigid sex over and over, but she had not touched it directly yet. She didn't want to simply touch.

Annette wanted to taste. This wasn't something she'd done much of, not out of distaste, but she'd been insecure in her technique.

This morning, she decided technique did not matter. She wanted to taste, so she would.

Carlo nearly came off the bed when Annette lapped at the tip of his penis with delicate little licks. Her hands were wrapped around his erection, making subtle movements up and down. Not enough to send him over the precipice, and he was grateful for that. Enough to turn a hardon into steel though.

Her mouth popped over his sex, taking him into her moist heat and Carlo shouted. The loud sound didn't shock her into stopping, but increased her efforts at exciting him. She'd taken him in her mouth before, but never with this abandon. Something had changed, but he was too excited to try to figure out what. Perhaps it was as simple as being husband and wife.

Ecstasy flowed through him, and he knew he was close. No matter how much she might be enjoying herself, he wasn't going to climax in her mouth.

His sweet wife was not ready for that. Many women never enjoyed the taste of a man's ejaculate.

Carlo pressed against Annette's shoulders. "Stop, *cara mia*."

Chapter Eighteen

Annette ignored his demand, sucking at his sex with delightful enthusiasm.

"Please, *bèdda*. Stop."

She came off his sex with a pop and swiped at her beautiful mouth, swollen from their kissing and what she'd just been doing. "Why?"

"I want to be inside your beautiful body when I come."

She thought about it, which turned him on even more. She was thinking what she wanted more and that idea that she'd been enjoying pleasuring him that much was as exciting as a touch.

"Okay." She scooted up his body until she straddled his thighs nearly kissing his erection with her feminine heat. "Hold yourself steady."

Carlo did, turned on by her sexual confidence.

She lowered herself onto his erection, her slick heat enveloping him as she pressed downward. He reached up and cupped her luscious rosy tipped breasts. She threw her head back, her gorgeous curvaceous body flushing with desire. Shifting back and forth, she rocked herself until he was fully seated inside her.

They both groaned.

Unable to stand the passivity any longer, Carlo began to thrust upward, one hand moving to her waist to hold her in place.

But Annette leaned forward and began her own pace. Their bodies came together with more force than he expected, but it felt good. Almost too good.

Annette's moan of pleasure and demand he do that again said she felt the same.

His climax was riding him hard, and Carlo knew he wasn't going to last many more thrusts, much less minutes. He shifted one hand so his thumb could press against her clitoris.

Her cry of delight was followed by a shimmy that about sent him over.

He rubbed her swollen nub, and she shifted her body for maximum pleasure, taking the pleasure he wanted to give and guiding it toward her own moment of ecstasy.

She looked down at him, her face flushed with pleasure. "I'm so close."

"Bèdda mia." He could get no other words out, her beauty so intense in that moment, it dazzled him.

Her eyes sparking like sapphires under a spotlight, Annette's body went tight above him and she cried out as her vaginal walls tightened around his sex. Carlo thrusted upward, coming so hard he shouted with the pleasure of it.

They moved together after, drawing aftershocks of ecstasy from each other's bodies before she collapsed on top of him. "How does it get better and better?"

"I do not know." No more than he understood why it was not all that great with other women anymore.

Though he was starting to get a glimmer.

After a leisurely breakfast and shower with more sexy times, Carlo asked Annette if she wanted to go into Dubrovnik. Eager to see the mixed architecture and explore the ancient streets of Old Town, Annette agreed.

"It's like Sicily, but not," she said as they walked in the Stradun with buildings on either side that had been built centuries ago.

"Both have similar cultural influences from Italy and Greece."

She nodded, delighted by the red tiled roofs and stone walled buildings, some with ornate columns and others more elegantly simple. "The weather is amazing too."

Sunny, but not too hot, it was the perfect day for walking down the limestone streets. They spent two hours in the Rector's Palace, which now housed the Cultural History Museum. Carlo held Annette's hand and they brought each other's attention to displays that caught their eyes.

It was so much like the past, when they had found each other's company easy and pleasurable, that Annette felt a sort of time displacement.

When they came back out into the sun, she squinted at the bright light and Carlo handed her a pair of designer sunglasses to put on. They were clearly women's glasses and meant for her.

"Thank you." She hadn't brought a pair with her, but he'd been prepared. "It's been wonderful, but everyone is closing for *pižolot*." She had been surprised by the afternoon nap similar to the Spanish *siesta* observed here. "There are so many more things I want to see. I think I could spend a year in this town alone, just soaking in the architecture, atmosphere and history."

"We can come back tomorrow. We have two weeks here, this time."

"This time?" she asked as they made their way to the SUV waiting for them.

"I bought the villa."

"You did?" It did have some things in it that didn't feel like they would be in a rental property, even one in use by billionaires. "The bedroom. It's done in the colors I told you I loved for a bedroom." The same colors she'd used when decorating her space when she'd gotten to Portland.

"I bought the house five years ago."

"Oh, Carlo." And the man still denied being a romantic. "I love it."

"I am glad. It is yours."

"What? No, it's not."

"I assure you, it is. You signed the deeds with the prenuptial agreement five years ago."

Which didn't say much for how closely she'd read that document back then. She blushed, knowing her father would be appalled if he knew.

She turned and threw her arms around him, kissing him soundly. "Thank you."

"You can thank me like that any time," he promised.

The following days fell into a pattern. After waking to make love, Annette and Carlo did touristy things, then in the evenings they took out the boat that was moored at the house's slip. She was not at all surprised to find out Carlo owned the mini yacht, but was stunned when she read the name *Sapphire* painted on the side.

He'd named it for her. Annette remembered how he used to say her eyes glowed like the blue precious stones, and her gut told her his intention had been to play on that connection. Or was that her heart?

Sometimes, Carlo worked while Annette lounged by the pool or read on the terrace. He was always solicitous and kind. Like with the sunglasses, he seemed to just know what Annette needed and make sure she got it.

He treated her like he valued her. He consulted her on how they should spend their days, and he'd even asked her if she wanted to live in the family home in Sicily, or get their own place.

Several generations of his family had lived in the mansion sized villa outside Palermo, but he was willing to buy another home for them, so she would feel comfortable. Annette had told him she had no trouble living with his parents.

Annette *liked* Valentina and Alceu. Equally importantly, she knew they liked her. She wouldn't hurt them for the world, and she thought having their oldest son break with tradition and move out would have done so.

Besides, the villa was big enough for Carlo, Annette and their children to have their own wing. Which she said to Carlo.

"*Sì.* We will have our own space." His expression was odd though.

"What?" she asked.

He looked at her like he didn't understand the question.

"You've got a strange look on your face," she explained.

"I was thinking about having more children with you."

"Good thoughts?" she quipped.

He indicated evidence of his arousal in his trousers with a flick of his masculine hand. "Very good thoughts."

Annette smiled contentedly, pleased that the idea of having more children with her turned him on like that. Which was probably another *throwback* reaction on her part, but then so was his visceral response to the idea.

Despite being okay with living in the Sicilian villa with his parents, Annette was glad they were still in New York when she and Carlo returned from the Dalmatian Coast.

She had a chance to settle into her new life without anyone else looking on.

If she didn't count the myriad staff, but like security, live in staff were an inevitable part of the life of wife to a billionaire businessman.

"What does that look mean?" Carlo asked, his hand reaching for her nape.

He was always touching her, and Annette loved it. She'd spent most of her life bereft of touch from loved ones and he seemed intent on making up for those barren years all at once.

Annette leaned into him, sliding her own arm around his trim waist. "I was just thinking that it's nice to settle into the villa without worrying what your parents think."

"And that amused you?" he asked as they headed out onto the terrace.

Carlo liked being outside as much as she did, and they had spent a lot of time relaxing together on a luxurious double lounger with a shade covering on their honeymoon. Well, Annette had relaxed, sometimes reading, sometimes napping.

Carlo had been on his phone, no doubt working, but he'd been there with her, and he was the one who would take her book from her hands and kiss her, or wake her from her dozing with the same.

"I was amused at my own lack of logic," she told him as they sat down on an outdoor sofa. It was a large corner shaped seating area, but they sat close together at the end with a chaise. She kicked off her sandals and put her feet up. "We're hardly without prying eyes, not with a whole villa full of staff."

"Does that bother you?" He put his arm around her shoulder, his fingers brushing back and forth over shoulders bared by her floral sundress.

Annette shivered, her nipples reacting to the light touch as if they were in the bedroom and not out on the terrace.

"No," she answered him, her tone husky.

"Papa and Mama will be returning early next month," Carlo said, like he was warning her.

Annette grinned. "I'm so glad things are going so well for Joyce and Fantino that they are able to do that. Besides, I can't wait to see them."

His parents treated her like a beloved, longed for daughter, just like they did Joyce, and Annette reveled in that kind of parental affection after a lifetime without it.

"*Bene.* I am glad."

"When do you return to the office?" she asked, dreading the answer and yet aware that their idyll could not last forever.

"Tomorrow."

"Oh." So soon.

"You are disappointed. Will you miss me?"

She nodded, seeing no reason to pretend otherwise. Her phone buzzed before she could give a verbal response. Annette looked down. Another text from her father. He wanted to know when they were going to have a formal reception to celebrate the wedding.

"That look is definitely not amusement," Carlo said.

Rather than explain, she showed him the phone.

Carlo swore succinctly. "How long has he been bothering you with this?" Rather than wait for her answer, he scrolled up in the text thread to check for himself and swore again, this time more inventively.

"I've been ignoring their calls and texts. I should have blocked their numbers." But they were her parents and she had felt wrong about doing that.

Again. Five years ago, she'd only blocked them for a few days, but they had been furious. Even though they didn't want her in the family, they expected her to be available to them when they needed something.

Boundaries. She still struggled with them, even after three years of therapy and five years in exile.

"I will speak to your father."

"No, it's my responsibility."

Carlo's jaw tautened, but he nodded.

He really was making every effort to prove that he had no desire to control her life.

Just this minute, she could wish he wasn't trying so hard. It would be so easy to let him field the call. Her father would never say the things to Carlo she knew he would say to her. But Annette wasn't weak. She could handle one uncomfortable phone call with her parents. After all, she'd survived their treatment most of her life.

"I'll go call him back," she said, getting up with reluctance.

Carlo's big body was tense with the need to act. "Are you sure you don't want me to make the call?"

Annette shook her head, unable to force out another verbal denial.

Annette had walked halfway around the house, on the wrap around terrace, looking for a private spot to make the call when it occurred to her that she was only putting off the unpleasant. She stopped and sat down on a bench that overlooked the olive grove to the side of the house.

This was as private as it was going to get.

Checking the time, and confirming it was neither too early nor too late, she dialed her father's number.

"It's about time you called," her father said by way of a greeting, his tone filled with annoyance and censure.

"I was on my honeymoon."

"Not that we were invited to your wedding," he replied with cold disapproval.

She wasn't going to feel guilty for that. "You made it clear you no longer consider me part of your family."

"Asking you to move so the scandal you caused could die down was not an excommunication from our family."

How easily he rewrote history to suit himself. Just like when he and her mom had rewritten history to say she was their daughter and not her biological father's. Had they followed that rewrite up with love and acceptance, Annette's life and perception of herself would be very different.

"First, I didn't cause that scandal. Lynette did," Annette said firmly. "Second, you didn't just ask me to move, you bribed an organization to transfer me to a job in another state. And you and mom refused to have me *home* for any holidays. That definitely qualifies as being kicked out of the family."

"You were at your sister's wedding and the baby's christening," he scoffed.

"Because Joyce never stopped seeing me as her sister."

"You cannot blame your poor choices on Lynette." Typical. Deflection when he had no answer for the truth.

"No, but I can blame her for feeding the media frenzy."

Her father started to say something, but Annette cut him off. Suddenly she was done, just done with parents who didn't care about her and a sister who actively disliked her. "Listen, there isn't going to be any reception."

Although maybe the Messinas wanted one? Annette would have to ask them. "I don't think. Carlo and I haven't talked about it."

"Of course, there will be a reception. Events like that are necessary for business."

"My marriage is not a business deal."

"What else could it be? Carlo married you to solidify his company's connection to mine. Even you should have enough intelligence to see that."

Annette knew why Carlo had married her and it had nothing to do with business. It had to do with the baby growing inside her, another tidbit she had yet to share with her parents. Maybe Joyce would let it slip and Annette could avoid another phone call like this one. Or not. She would fight one battle at a time.

"Even me?" she demanded, tired of the put downs. "Which of your children was it who won an academic scholarship for college? Oh, right, that would be me. I'm plenty intelligent, dad, but I'm not a pushover. Not anymore."

"Is that how you justify not inviting your parents to your wedding?" he asked scathingly, "Telling yourself you're not a pushover. You owe us. We raised you."

"If you had ever bothered to even try to love me, that might mean something, but you were paid for the services you rendered. That precious business of yours wouldn't exist but for your agreement to *take me in*."

Her father was silent for long seconds, clearly unsure how to take this new less than tolerant attitude from her. She'd never fought them on anything important.

"I'm sure the Messinas were there," her father finally said.

"Yes, they were." As Joyce had been, but saying so would have been petty and Annette was not that. Firm? Yes. Determined to stop being the Cinderella figure in her family's life? Yes. But she had no desire to hurt anyone unnecessarily.

"So, we should have been invited as well."

"No." She wasn't going to bother going into the why again. If he didn't understand now, he never would.

"Carlo isn't going to be your golden goose business partner," she warned her father, finding his claim that her husband had married her for the business connection ludicrous.

It was clear who benefited most from their business connections, and it wasn't her husband.

Chapter Nineteen

"Have you been poisoning him against me?" Annette's father demanded with rancor.

"He was appalled by both your and mom's behavior at the lawyer's office. When I told him about me being adopted and how you only did it to get money from your wealthier, older brother, he wasn't all that impressed either."

"That's ridiculous. We were on his side. You can't tell me he took that against us." Typical of her father to completely ignore any reference to her adoption, or the reason for it.

Yes, they'd been on what they considered Carlo's side, just like they had been five years ago. She was their daughter, but she didn't matter. Her feelings didn't matter.

She wanted to hang up, but she had one last thing she had to say. "I'm pregnant. I will take your congratulations as spoken," she said sarcastically before her father could speak. "Whether you are allowed into my family's life will be determined by your choices. How you choose to treat me. Whether you attempt to play the same favorites with your grandchildren that you have your own children."

Whatever their reasons, they'd adopted her, darn it. And they had forced her to recognize them as her parents. Now, they could either recognize her as their daughter with all rights and privileges, or they could stay well out of her life.

"You think you've landed yourself in clover, don't you? Carlo Messina only married you because you're pregnant with my grandchild."

Man, it had taken mere minutes for her father to change his tack on that one. First his business, now *his* grandchild. Not *her* baby. What a narcissist.

"You've insinuated yourself in his life, but he'll see you for what you are." What her dad thought that was, he left unsaid.

But she'd had a lifetime to figure it out and it wasn't something good.

"What I am is a loving person who will be a great mom, because there was a time many years ago that I had one." She would hold onto that memory always and they could not take it away from her, even if they'd managed to erase the connection between her and her biological father. "And if nothing else, you and mom have taught me important lessons about raising all my children with the same love and affection."

A hand was suddenly in front of her, open like ready to take the phone, but not reaching for it.

She stared at that hand and then looked up into her husband's face. His handsome features were cast in fury.

How much of their conversation had he heard? Had he been there the whole time? Annette's phone was a cheap model that bled a lot of noise. No such thing as a truly private phone call if anyone else was around.

"May I speak now?" he asked politely.

She almost laughed but stifled the sound and handed him the phone. She'd said what she needed to.

"Floyd, this is Carlo," her husband said in a chilled tone, so different than the one he used with her.

The sound of her father's voice, which had been raised in a litany of the usual complaints against her, cut off abruptly.

"Listen carefully. If you ever speak in this cutting way to my wife again, not only will we cut you from our lives, but I will cut all business ties with you as well."

Annette stood up from the bench and stepped away to the edge of the terrace, not wanting to hear her father's response.

Though she couldn't miss Carlo's next words. "No, there will be no further business dealings, but I will not cancel current contracts. That is as far as my generosity takes me."

Carlo and her father spoke for only a few moments more before Carlo informed the other man that all communication from the Hudsons needed to come to him, not be directed toward Annette. When he looked at her, like asking if that was okay, she nodded.

She was done. Annette would not waste any more energy trying to earn love or respect from her adopted family and she frankly never wanted to see her biological father again. Not that he'd shown any desire to build a relationship over the years.

She just knew *she* no longer wanted to, either.

She had a new family, and she was going to concentrate all her love and energy on them.

That night, when they made love, Annette said the words out loud.

"I love you, Carlo." She needed him to know.

He was on top this time, setting the rhythm. His grey eyes dark with passion, he shushed her. "Shh. Just feel. No talking."

Annette told herself it didn't matter, that he deserved to know she loved him. Carlo had given her a family who loved and accepted her, a family she adored as well. He was such a good man. Yes, a little controlling and used to getting his way, but he listened and stepped back when he needed to.

She said it again when ecstasy took them and ignored the echo of silence that came after.

Carlo lay in the darkness, awake and thinking, his precious wife lost to slumber beside him. They had made love more than once tonight, exhausting, but also eliciting word of love.

Did she mean them? Did she love him again? Still?

He hadn't said the words back, but for the first time he accepted he felt them. Why had he fought the admission so hard?

Because five years ago, he'd believed himself in love and loved in return only to be humiliated and rejected on his wedding day. His pride had not allowed him to acknowledge the deep wound, not even to his brother.

Now that he had better perspective on the past, Carlo knew Annette had meant the words when she said them five years ago. So, why did he doubt them now?

Because of the baby. She'd married him for the baby's sake.

Wasn't that what she thought about him? That he'd only wanted to marry her because she was pregnant?

Who was the genius that told her he only wanted sex to work her out of his system?

That would be him.

But he loved her. And he had to tell her. Would she be upset if he woke her up to do so?

He could wait for the morning, surely.

Carlo lay, rigid, fighting the need to wake his wife with tender kisses and whisper sweet words of adoration in her ear.

Annette shifted and then groaned. "I have to pee," she said, as if talking to herself.

Never had a bodily function been so welcome by Carlo. "I would like to tell you something when you're done."

She jerked as if startled. "Carlo? You're awake?" she asked, sounding more alert herself.

"I am."

"And you want to tell me something? In the middle of the night?"

"It can wait for your bladder."

"Baby more like. It's like she rolls right onto my bladder every other hour."

They'd found out the baby was a girl at the OB's visit just before their wedding. Joyce and Annette had been ecstatic, promising each other their daughters would be the best of friends. Just like sisters.

Carlo replayed that sweet memory in his head as he waited for his wife to return to their bed.

When Annette came back into the bedroom, Carlo had turned on a lamp and was sitting up, his expression filled with an emotion she was afraid to name.

"You didn't say it earlier, when I did," she blurted. "Or five years ago. You never said it."

"Five years ago, I planned to say it on our wedding night."

"You did?" she asked faintly.

"Sì."

"And tonight?"

"I was still fighting admitting it to myself."

"Why?"

"Because if I loved you, then I'd been lying to myself for five years and telling real whoppers since Joyce and Fantino's wedding."

Annette climbed back into the bed, letting Carlo pull her right onto his knees so they were practically eye level. He tucked the blankets around her with solicitous care.

"You're always so attentive, doing stuff like that. I just thought you were *that* guy, you know?"

"That guy?" he asked, leaning in a little to inhale her scent.

He did that sometimes. She did the same thing. No other man she'd ever met smelled quite like Carlo and it wasn't just his cologne.

"You know, the good guy. The honorable guy. The man who will marry the mother of his baby even if he doesn't trust her to keep her promises."

"But I do trust you *bèdda mia*."

"Yes, I believe you, only when we got married, I was sure it was all about the baby."

"Our baby is a gift, but our marriage was all about you. It has always been all about you."

"Not for anyone else. Never for anyone else."

"Your family do not deserve you."

"But *Famigghia esti famigghia*," she said, quoting the Sicilian saying. Family was family. "If they can be decent, even if they aren't ever loving, I'll allow them space in my life and that of our child."

"And if they are not, I will destroy your father and see them bankrupt."

"I think you're kidding. You *are* joking, aren't you?"

Carlo just shrugged. "I did not wake you to talk about your family."

"You didn't wake me at all. Our baby did that." Then the baby kicked and she gasped. "Here..." She grabbed Carlo's hand and placed it against her hard abdomen, though it was still a pretty small baby bump. "Feel."

"I can feel her," Carlo said with awe.

"Isn't it amazing?"

He just nodded, his eyes shiny.

This man. He did her in with emotion. "You said you had something to say to me, when I woke up to pee," she reminded him.

"Ah, yes. I wanted to wake you so badly, I think I willed our daughter to move onto your bladder."

Annette laughed and shook her head. "Whatever you say."

"I say that I love with all that is within me for all of this life and beyond."

For a moment, she was so overcome, she could not speak. "That's a lot of love," she said finally.

"There is no man who loves another more than I love you," he assured her in all seriousness.

And Annette just soaked it in. All that love, all that assurance. "I love you. I always have. I am so sorry I ran five years ago."

"I am so sorry I was such an ass that you felt the need to run."

"Next time you're an ass, I'll stand and fight."

"You're so sure there will be a next time?"

"There has to be. Otherwise, you would be perfect, and I cannot live up to, or with, perfection."

"We shall see."

She smiled and then kissed him, not bothered at all when that led to more. Later, they lay entwined and whispered words of love until they fell asleep together.

Her dreams were sweet and she woke beside the man she loved and the man she now knew loved her.

She looked at the clock and then started. "Aren't you supposed to be at the office?"

"I am playing hooky. We are celebrating."

"What are we celebrating?"

"Being in love."

They spent the day doing just that, but it didn't stop with a day. Carlo thought that their love should be celebrated often and well.

Annette agreed. It was an amazing gift.

EPILOGUE

The evening of their first anniversary, Annette met Carlo on the terrace outside their bedroom with a sheaf of papers.

"What is this?" he asked.

"I've got a contract for you to sign."

"Do you?" He took the papers and began reading, his laughter ringing soon thereafter.

Annette settled onto his lap, enjoying how much easier it was to do so now than it had been six months before. She'd barely shown for the first five months and then ballooned to a basketball sized tummy at supersonic speed.

Carlo had spent the last months of her pregnancy kissing her stretch marks and telling her how beautiful they were, a mark of her motherhood. Now, their adorable little Joy was six months old and wonder of wonders, sleeping through the night.

"What's so funny?" she asked him, as if she did not know.

"This reads more like a teenaged girl's sex fantasies than a contract," he told her, echoing her words from a fateful day that had brought them here. He went serious. "But it's this final set of articles I can't live without."

Annette had poured her love onto those pages, promising the many ways she would show it to him throughout their life.

"I will only sign this if I can add some clauses of my own."

"Of course. It's a love contract after all and love is both give and take."

"In this case, I want to give it to you. Every day for all of our lives."

And that is what he did.

THE END

With more than 10 million copies of my books in print worldwide (Isn't that wild?), I'm an award winning and USA Today bestselling author with over 90 published books. My stories have been translated for sale all over the world and after a long career in traditional publishing, I've gone indie. I am loving the freedom to write the stories both me and my readers enjoy the most. My new steamy mafia romance series, Syndicate Rules features the morally gray alpha heroes and spice I love to write. I write contemporary, historical and paranormal romance. Some of my books have action adventure and intrigue. All of them are spicy and deeply emotional. I'm a voracious reader and love to talk about both my books and those I've read (or should read...good recs are always welcome) on social media. Welcome to my world where love conquers all, but not easily!

For info on my books and series extras, visit my website:
www.lucymonroe.com

Follow me on Social Media:
Facebook: LucyMonroe.Romance
Instagram: lucymonroeromance
Pinterest: lucymonroebooks
goodreads: Lucy Monroe
YouTube: @LucyMonroeBooks
TikTok: lucymonroeauthor

ALSO BY LUCY MONROE

Syndicate Rules

CONVENIENT MAFIA WIFE
URGENT VOWS
DEMANDING MOB BOSS
RUTHLESS ENFORCER
BRUTAL CAPO
FORCED VOWS

Mercenaries & Spies

READY, WILLING & AND ABLE
SATISFACTION GUARANTEED
DEAL WITH THIS
THE SPY WHO WANTS ME
WATCH OVER ME
CLOSE QUARTERS
HEAT SEEKER

CHANGE THE GAME
WIN THE GAME

Passionate Billionaires & Royalty

THE MAHARAJAH'S BILLIONAIRE HEIR
BLACKMAILED BY THE BILLIONAIRE
HER OFF LIMITS PRINCE
CINDERELLA'S JILTED BILLIONAIRE
HER GREEK BILLIONAIRE
SCORSOLINI BABY SCANDAL
THE REAL DEAL
WILD HEAT (Connected to Hot Alaska Nights - Not a Billionaire)
HOT ALASKA NIGHTS

3 Brides for 3 Bad Boys Trilogy
RAND, COLTON & CARTER

Harlequin Presents

THE GREEK TYCOON'S ULTIMATUM
THE ITALIAN'S SUITABLE WIFE
THE BILLIONAIRE'S PREGNANT MISTRESS
THE SHEIKH'S BARTERED BRIDE
THE GREEK'S INNOCENT VIRGIN
BLACKMAILED INTO MARRIAGE
THE GREEK'S CHRISTMAS BABY
WEDDING VOW OF REVENGE
THE PRINCE'S VIRGIN WIFE
HIS ROYAL LOVE-CHILD
THE SCORSOLINI MARRIAGE BARGAIN
THE PLAYBOY'S SEDUCTION
PREGNANCY OF PASSION
THE SICILIAN'S MARRIAGE ARRANGEMENT
BOUGHT: THE GREEK'S BRIDE
TAKEN: THE SPANIARD'S VIRGIN
HOT DESERT NIGHTS
THE RANCHER'S RULES
FORBIDDEN: THE BILLIONAIRE'S
VIRGIN PRINCESS
HOUSEKEEPER TO THE MILLIONAIRE
HIRED: THE SHEIKH'S SECRETARY MISTRESS
VALENTINO'S LOVE-CHILD
THE LATIN LOVER 2-IN-1 with
THE GREEK TYCOON'S INHERITED BRIDE
THE SHY BRIDE
THE GREEK'S PREGNANT LOVER
FOR DUTY'S SAKE
HEART OF A DESERT WARRIOR
NOT JUST THE GREEK'S WIFE
ONE NIGHT HEIR
PRINCE OF SECRETS

MILLION DOLLAR CHRISTMAS PROPOSAL
SHEIKH'S SCANDAL
AN HEIRESS FOR HIS EMPIRE
A VIRGIN FOR HIS PRIZE
2017 CHRISTMAS CODA: The Greek Tycoons
KOSTA'S CONVENIENT BRIDE
THE SPANIARD'S PLEASURABLE VENGEANCE
AFTER THE BILLIONAIRE'S WEDDING VOWS
QUEEN BY ROYAL APPOINTMENT
HIS MAJESTY'S HIDDEN HEIR
THE COST OF THEIR ROYAL FLING

Anthologies & Novellas

SILVER BELLA
DELICIOUS: Moon Magnetism
by Lori Foster, et. al.
HE'S THE ONE: Seducing Tabby
by Linda Lael Miller, et. al.
THE POWER OF LOVE: No Angel
by Lori Foster, et. al.
BODYGUARDS IN BED:
Who's Been Sleeping in my Brother's Bed?
by Lucy Monroe et. al.

Historical Romance

ANNABELLE'S COURTSHIP
The Langley Family Trilogy
TOUCH ME, TEMPT ME & TAKE ME
MASQUERADE IN EGYPT

Paranormal Romance

Children of the Moon Novels
MOON AWAKENING
MOON CRAVING

MOON BURNING
DRAGON'S MOON
ENTHRALLED anthology: Ecstasy Under the Moon
WARRIOR'S MOON
VIKING'S MOON
DESERT MOON
HIGHLANDER'S MOON

Montana Wolves
COME MOONRISE
MONTANA MOON

Printed in Great Britain
by Amazon